Lime Pickled

and Other Stories

Marc de Faoite

ISBN: 978-1-913584-15-3 PAPERBACK

A Leopard Print book

First published in Great Britain in 2023 by Leopard Print.

To my parents, Noel and Siobhan,
for the gift of a human life and so much more.

In memory of Elaine Byrne

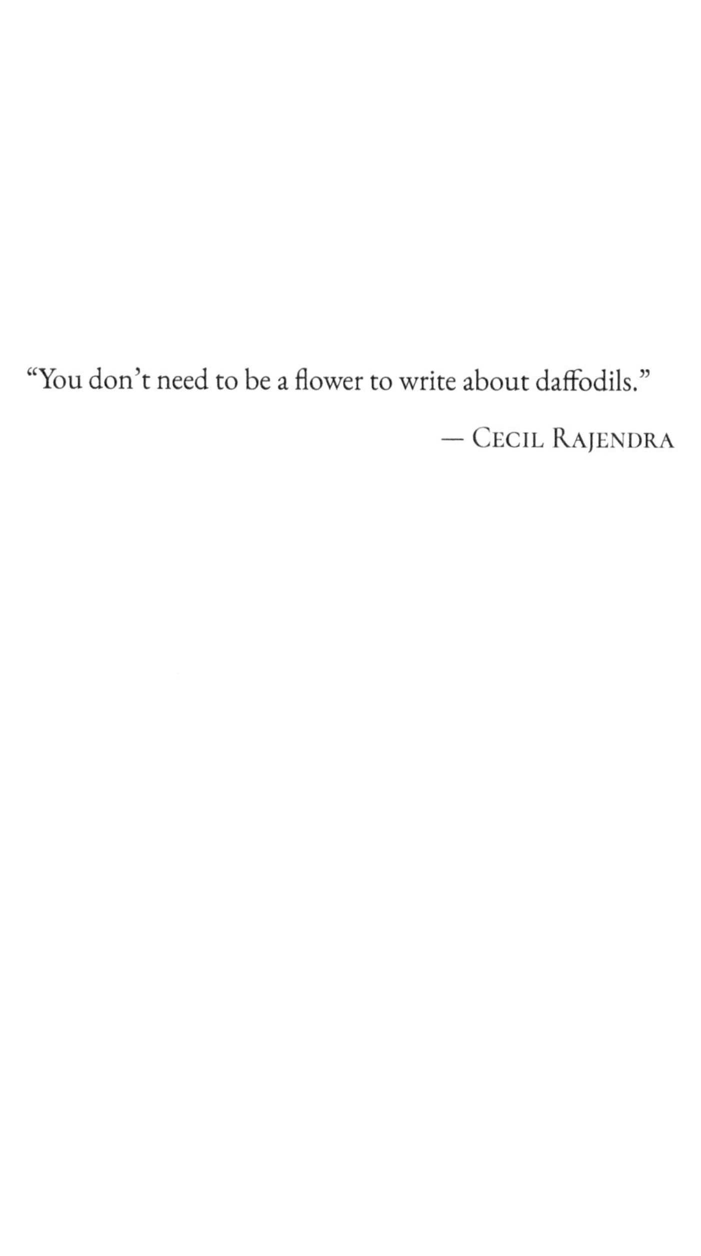

"You don't need to be a flower to write about daffodils."

— Cecil Rajendra

Contents

Red Monkey Sam

Every time I opened the kitchen window Sam came in. He paused to bare his teeth and hiss at me, then ran wild through the house, climbing over furniture, opening cupboards, biting into anything that looked edible. And those teeth - as long and sharp as needles. Proper scared the life out of me, they did.

"You must shoot him," said Encik Azan.

Easy for him to say. While I didn't want him in my house – the monkey I mean, not our neighbour – I certainly didn't want to kill him. Besides, I knew Encik Azan was one of those bossy men who think they can go around telling women what to do. I wasn't having none of it and was starting to get right peeved off about how this geezer always seemed to show up as soon as my Andy was out of the house.

"But this is how we do. Otherwise how to stop him?"

"Well, couldn't we just catch him somehow and take him away? Put him in a box and drive him to the other side of the island?"

"He come back. He likes it here. This island not so big. This monkey clever. He knows where you live."

Andy reckoned Sam must have lived here before the house

was built. Whatever drew him, the monkey just kept coming back.

THE SOLE of one of my shoes was coming undone. That's what happens when you buy cheap shoes and get caught out by surprise in a monsoon storm. But I'm not one for throwing out a perfectly good pair of shoes, cheap or not. That's the problem with the world nowadays, everything disposable.

I bought a tube of Superglue at the little supermarket at the crossroads. It's a messy place, stuff all piled up higgledy-piggledy, but if you root around you can find nearly everything you need, except ginger-nut biscuits. Andy likes them with a cup of tea. Have to keep them in a box in the fridge or the ants will have them, or the humidity will make them go soft. They stopped stocking them about six months ago. I asked Puan Azizah to get them in again.

"No point," she smiled, putting dimples in her chubby cheeks. "All you Mat Salleh buy them and there are none left for anyone else."

I thought about that for a moment and was going to say something, but instead I just shook my head, paid for the superglue and left, reminding myself to get gingernuts at the Chinese supermarket on my next trip to town.

THE SUPERGLUE WAS on the kitchen counter, still in its plastic and cardboard wrapping. So much packaging for a tiny tube of glue. Madness. The world these days, honestly. I was working my way down my to-do list, sweating after pushing a damp mop around the kitchen floor. I opened the window in the hope that the breeze would dry the lino. Of course the moment I opened the window, in jumps the bloody monkey.

I had taken to calling him Sam. I don't know why, it just

seemed like a name that suited him. So Sam came barging past me, started opening cupboards, pulling out all my pots and pans. I suppose the shiny plastic wrapping caught his eye. He ripped the packaging open with his teeth, and pulled out the little yellow tube of glue, like taking a nut from a shell. It usually takes me ten minutes of pulling and struggling to open those packets until I give up and throw them at Andy in frustration. Andy is practical. He uses a box cutter to open everything, a trick he learned when we used to buy CDs. They were always bloody impossible to unwrap.

I suppose he thought the tube of glue was some sort of fruit – Sam I mean, not Andy. He looked at it, sniffed it, then popped it in his mouth.

"No," I shouted. I had a sudden vision of Sam with his teeth and lips permanently stuck together and wasting away from starvation and thirst. Even though the thought of it was terrible, I couldn't help but laugh.

Take it from me, don't ever laugh at a monkey. Don't even smile. When they see your teeth they take it as a threat. Sam lunged at me. I'd never faced him down or threatened him before, but I still had the mop in my hands, so I suppose it was natural to lash out, but Sam was fast and dodged around me, running into the living room, where he smashed some of the porcelain figurines I had brought over to remind us of home.

Lately I don't want to be reminded of our old lives back there, so losing the ornaments was no big deal. In fact I used the mop handle to smash a few more, knowing that if Andy asked, I could just blame it on the monkey. Crash went the little blue boy with curls, joined by his pink sister. I wanted to smash everything. Little horses and bunnies and dogs shattered on impact. The owl and the pussycat in their beautiful pea-green boat bounced off the floor, but didn't break. I flung it at Sam, missed, but it exploded into pieces that I kept finding for days afterwards. "No more dancing by the light of the moon for you two," I shouted. I don't know what came over me. Anyway, I frightened the monkey good and proper. Frightened myself and all, if truth be told. Off he went back through the kitchen and out the window.

I found the tube of glue while I was sweeping up bits of broken porcelain. It was a miracle it hadn't burst. I still have it in a drawer in the kitchen. I used to take it out and show the little teeth marks on the soft metal tube to visitors.

When we moved here first we invited almost every white person we met over for dinner. Very few of them ever invited us back. No loss I can tell you. Well fond of the bottle most of them are. I'm not saying that I don't like a tipple myself now and then, but there's a limit. To be honest it doesn't get any easier as I get older. These days the hangovers seem to come on even before I'm drunk, so what's the point? It's just straight to the punishment. So between one thing and the other, we don't mix much these days. We'll nod and say hello, or have a little chat if we run into anyone we know at the supermarket, but otherwise, we pretty much keep ourselves to ourselves. Besides, you get bored of hearing stories about their bloody sailboats, as if that's the only thing that matters in life. People like them can't accept people like us having money. They always want to know what school Andy went to, or what he did back home. We came here to get away from that sort of thing. If he's pushed Andy just mumbles something about a job in a bank. Course, he never says that the job lasted just one night and gave us enough cash to retire on, and then some. Best keep a low profile. Anyone asks Andy his name, he always says Frank. I tell them I'm May, though really I'm June. We might be on the other side of the world, but you can't be too careful.

"Auntie!"

Old Encik Azan was standing at the bottom of the steps up to the veranda. He was holding a sort of metal cage with a wire hoop on it.

"I bring this for your monkey. It is a trap and you will catch him inside. You must open it like this," he said, opening the spring-loaded door. "Then you put a banana on this hook. Push the hook all the way in, top to bottom, then when monkey try the take the banana the door will close." He let the metal door slam shut with a sudden crash.

"But then what can we do? You said the monkey will come back."

"Then what we do is we bring the cage to the sea and tie a big rock."

"You mean you drown the monkey? But that's awful."

"Yes, if we don't shoot the monkey we drown the monkey. But wait, there is one other way."

"I'm not sure I want to know another way to kill a monkey, thank you very much."

"No, I know you white people do not like to kill wild things, so I bring you this."

From the folds of his long shirt, Encik Azan produced an aerosol can. Probably had it tucked into the hem of his sarong. He handed it to me. The lid was bright red.

"Red paint?"

"Yes. This. When you catch the monkey, you must spray on him. Make him all red. Then when you set him free he will go away. Other monkeys will not accept him."

I talked it over with Andy that evening when he came back from his cycle. He was breathless and sweat was pouring down his face.

"Was you waiting long my love? Ran out of steam, didn't I."

He looked tired. Neither of us is getting any younger. We'll probably die on this island. We certainly can't risk going back. I told Andy that if I go first I want to be cremated at the Hindu temple up by the rubber plantation. A few old expats have been sent off that way. I used to think death was something terrible, but some days I'm so tired that I feel it will be a rest.

Still, we have a few more years in us yet and Andy's cycling keeps him fit. He has a body of a man 15 years younger, so I'm not going to complain, am I? You're only as old as the man you feel, as they say.

Once he'd had his shower and guzzled a bottle of water we sat down to watch the sunset. It's like a ritual we have. We started the very first day we moved to this house. It's our time together. Most days we don't even talk, just sit and watch the sunset in silence and sip our drinks, but this evening I tell Andy about Encik Azan's visit and the spray can of red paint.

"Can't do any harm to try," said Andy.

The next day we set up the trap in the kitchen and left the window open. Within minutes we heard the snap of the cage door spring shut and a surprised shriek from poor little Sam.

Andy picked up the cage by the hoop and brought it outdoors, while Sam jumped around hissing and grunting.

"Heavy bastard. Hard to carry with him moving around like that."

My heart went out to him – Sam that is. Well to Andy as well I suppose but in a different way. He brought Sam to the end of the garden, down by the bougainvillaea. I followed along with the spray can and passed it to Andy.

"I'm not bloody doing it," he said, handing the paint back to me. "This was your idea, not mine."

"It was Encik Azan's idea," I said. "Anyways you always say painting's a man's job."

"Yeah, but I meant painting walls or doors. Never said nothing about no bloody monkeys."

I responded with a silent pout.

"Oh, give me the bloody thing then," said Andy, snatching the aerosol from my hand. I had to turn away to hide a victorious smile.

"Step back," he said. "Don't want you painted red as well, do we?"

I did as I was told and Andy shook the can making that rattling sound that spray cans always make. Sam was quieter now but kept looking from Andy to me and back again. Andy pushed down on the little white button. The hissing sound of the aerosol was drowned out by Sam's shrieks. You could tell the poor thing was terrified. Andy threw down the can in disgust. Sam was still screaming, but he just had a red stripe down the front of his chest.

"This ain't right," Andy said, shaking his head. "You deal with it." Then he stormed off back to the house.

I stood looking at poor Sam trying to wipe off the paint, but getting his tiny grey hands and mouth all red instead.

One nice thing about Andy is he can never stay angry for long. It's just not in his nature. While I might simmer for hours Andy's tantrums are usually short and swift, over almost as soon as begun. Within minutes he was back again. He had a bowl, a plastic-wrapped pan of Gardenia bread, the wholemeal one, because the white one is awful and is full of sugar and preservatives. As well as the bowl and the bread he had a bottle.

"Brandy," he said. "Let's knock the little bugger out cold."

Sam eyed Andy warily, sniffing the air as he watched him break the bread into small chunks. Then he poured the best part of half a bottle of brandy on top.

"If this won't quieten him down, nothing will," said Andy. I thought of mentioning the packet of Valium I keep in the bathroom cabinet - amazing that you can just buy the stuff over the counter here – but I decided to see how the booze worked first.

The trick was keeping Sam in the cage while opening the door wide enough to put the bowl inside. Andy puffed himself up big and roared at Sam, showing his teeth and rattling the cage. Sam crouched in the corner trying to make himself small, suitably intimidated by my Alpha-Male husband, then Andy quickly opened the spring-loaded door and slipped the bowl of boozy bread inside.

At first Sam didn't move. He stayed in the corner, watching us. You could see he was frightened. I felt a lump in my throat, but at the same time, told myself that we were doing the right thing, that it was better for Sam than being shot or drowned. We backed away to make him feel less threatened and after a minute or so he crept forward to investigate his brandy-spiked bread. After one or two tentative sniffs he took a handful of the mush and slurped it into his mouth. I swear I saw a tremor run through his little body, then a devious gleam light up in his eyes. He took more of the bread, and then more and soon he was properly drunk. He finished the bowl with his head lowered inside, licking it clean of every last drop. Then he let out a loud belch and fell onto his back with his head moving from side to side and a little string of drool running down the side of his mouth. For a moment I thought we had killed him, but then he rolled over and soon we could tell by his regular breathing that he was asleep.

Andy crept forward, armed with the aerosol, got up close and opened fire. This time Sam hardly reacted. He moaned and coughed a little, but was too drunk to care what was going on. Andy kicked the cage over; Sam's little body rolling over inside. Then Andy painted the rest of him red. I should have gone for the camera, but didn't even think of it at the time.

We let Sam sleep it off for a bit, then Andy opened the cage and lifted it, letting Sam flop to the ground. After a moment or two he stirred and staggered to his feet. It took him a few tries. He stared at us in confusion, then turned and made for the forest. We watched him try to climb a tree, but halfway up he fell down. He tried another tree with a similar result. In the end he just slunk away, his bright red coat of paint visible through the undergrowth for quite a distance until finally he was lost from sight.

Silver Spoons

"Prema. We need to talk."

"Yes, Madam," said Prema, suddenly flustered by the unfamiliar harshness in Mrs Hutchinson's voice.

"About the silverware, Prema."

"Silverware, Madam?"

"Don't you play coy with me, young lady. How long have you been with us now?"

"Four years, Madam. April five years starting."

"Indeed. Four years and more. Haven't we always been kind to you during that time?"

Prema felt the blood rush from her pounding heart towards her face. She blinked back tears, swallowed the uncomfortable lump that had appeared in her throat, suddenly aware of the sound of the ceiling fan stirring the humid air, its feeble breeze providing no relief.

"Yes, Madam, very kind. Very kind. You have been like mother to me."

"Like mother, indeed, the very words. Took you in, gave you a home, fed you, clothed you, shared our food with you. Our good fortune has been your good fortune. And this is how you repay us?"

Prema couldn't control her quivering lip, couldn't trust herself to speak without breaking down completely. Without breaking apart. So she said nothing, and just lowered her head, which Mrs Hutchinson apparently took as an admission of guilt.

"IT'S MY TURN," whined Jeremy.

"But there's only one left," said Christopher.

Their voices echoed strangely back at them as both boys leaned over the circular stonework of the well. Their 1950s haircuts, the perennial short-back-and-sides, made inverted wedges of their jug-eared heads as they peered down into the darkness. The well was too deep for the light to reach the surface of the water. There wasn't even a reflected glimmer at the bottom of the blackness.

"But you did it last time."

"We'll do it together then," said Christopher cheerily. "I'm the oldest, so I decide."

"That's not fair. I'm going to tell Mother that you wouldn't let me have my turn."

"No telling Mother anything about this, you hear? Alright, you do it then. But you have to be very quiet. And you have to spin it right."

Jeremy took the spoon and reached out as far as he could.

"You have to drop it down the centre, otherwise it won't work."

"I know, I know. I'm not bloody stupid."

"And face it downwards so the wind catches it, or else it won't spin."

"I already told you I know how to do it."

Both boys fell silent. Christopher stood close to his little brother, ready to catch him if he should lean too far. Jeremy dropped the spoon.

It fell, spinning, rotating on multiple axes, its bright metallic sheen winking on and off. As it fell it made a strange unearthly whirring sound, created by some bizarre effect of the acoustics of the well. For a fraction of a moment the spoon sang like a tuning fork, before ending with a tiny distant splash that echoed against the dark stonework like a disappointed sigh.

Both boys hung there, faces towards the darkness. Time had stopped. Then they began to breathe again. They became aware of the hardness of the stonework cutting across their bellies, and pushed themselves back into the world that existed beyond the small black circle that had so absorbed them.

"Well that's that," said Christopher, dusting off his hands and the tufts of moss that clung to the front of his shirt.

The boys walked back towards the house, following the worn trail that cut a dark brown swathe through the lush lalang, the rough grass taller than either of the young boys. The whine of the cicadas from the nearby trees, strident as the torrid heat, invisible birds calling out in whoops and chirps, barely noticed by the boys, these background noises as natural and normal to them as they were foreign to their mother.

"Can we not try with the knives and forks?" asked Jeremy, trailing behind his older brother.

"It wouldn't work. They wouldn't resist the air in the same way. It'd be just like dropping stones or sticks."

"They'd drop quicker than sticks though, wouldn't they?"

"They would, yes."

"I'm hungry."

"You're always hungry."

"Yes. Maybe Prema made chapatis. I'd love a chapati now."

"With melted butter."

"With melted butter and strawberry jam."

"Mother, where is Prema?" asked Jeremy. "She's not in the kitchen and I'm ravenous."

"We looked out in the hen house, we thought she might be collecting eggs, but we couldn't find her anywhere," said Christopher. "We even knocked on the door of her room, but she didn't answer. Do you think she's gone to visit the tappers?"

"Sit down both of you. I will make you sandwiches."

"Can we not have chapatis?"

"There are no chapatis."

"Why? Didn't Prema make chapatis today?"

"No. No, she didn't. And she won't be making any, any other day either. Prema is gone."

"She's gone? Where did she go? Is she going to tap rubber now with the other workers?"

"Perhaps. We'll let your father decide that. In any case she won't be living with us anymore."

"But why Mother, why?" asked Jeremy, almost on the verge of tears. He was too young to remember life before Prema. She had always been there.

"Because she did a very bad thing. Very bad."

"What did she do?" asked Christopher cautiously.

"She stole the silver spoons. All of them. I don't know how she got rid of them, I searched her room, but they are gone. We can't have a thief living among us. She's lucky I didn't report her to the police. If I did she'd be in prison now for sure."

"In prison?" asked Jeremy.

"Yes, but she's not. It's more than she deserves, but I gave her the chance to make a new start somewhere else. Sometimes I think I'm too kind-hearted by far. Too kind-hearted for my own good. That's why people take advantage. Too kind by far."

Christopher locked eyes with Jeremy. He looked back knowingly, and both boys sealed a pact of silence that would bind the brothers for close to forty years.

That night Jeremy dreamt of Prema kneading dough, locked up, behind bars, condemned to make chapatis for all her fellow prisoners. In the bed beside him, Christopher, thrashed about, tangling himself in the thin sheet, dreaming the same dream he would dream for years to come. He fell into the darkness, toppling at speed, the air rushing around his ears making it impossible for him to scream, even long after he had left the tropical climes of his childhood for the colder countries he had read about in storybooks, waking with a gasp, bathed in sweat, wondering what had ever become of Prema and if she knew he was to blame, wondering if anyone had ever found the secret trove of silver glistening in the silent water at the bottom of the well.

Floodbaby

She watched her husband try to light a candle. The hopeful flame flickered in the cross draft before extinguishing itself, again, leaving wavering imprints of retinal ghosts floating superimposed upon the darkness. Wind rattled the windows. A dog howled outside. How frightened and sodden the poor animal must be. The power had cut out an hour earlier. The internet was down. No phone signal either. She pictured her neighbours cowering from the storm too. Or maybe they had the good fortune or forethought to equip themselves with battery-powered lamps and a gas cooking stove. The baby shifted inside her, agitated in its liquid world, unsettled by the storm as well. Lightning cracked the darkness in eye-blink flashes, illuminating the plainness of the room. Flashbulb snapshots of the simple wooden table. The blank whitewashed walls. The darkly reflective stacked rectangles of uncurtained louvred windows. Sometimes several pulsing strobes echoed light through the electric air. Raindrops, leaking in percussive stutters from the tired tin roof into a worn blue plastic pail. She wondered if the child, her child, could hear the hammering rain. What would it sound like? She placed her palms over her ears, swapping storm sounds for a deep internal rumbling. The muffled uneven rhythm of her respiration.

She strained to distinguish a hint of heartbeat. The shifting syncopation of two beating hearts. She listened for a long time, calming the baby through telepathy, her breath catching whenever the lightning made its way through her closed eyelids, somehow even brighter in the constricted confines of her skull. She opened her eyes again to the dark room, lowered her palms from her ears to her belly, slowed her breath, counting and lengthening the exhale, counting the gaps between the noisy thunder rumble and the flashing light.

The bolted light struck with a simultaneous bang. No interval to count. An unworldly creaking groan was followed by the sibilant susurration of a million leaves as a nearby tree crashed to the ground. Perhaps the mango tree, perhaps the tamarind. Her husband, unwilling or unable to picture which, opened the front door to assess the loss and was immediately soaked as sideways rain blasted into the house. He had to lean with his back and push with his legs against the gale to close the door.

He had made the door himself, sawing and planing the wood, nailing and doweling and gluing the homemade planks. It was a good door. Solid. He was useful with his hands. She had always liked that about him. Some men were all talk, but he did things, made things. He had built the table and the chairs as well. Their bed. Shelves. Solid unpretentious furniture, much like the man himself. He would be a good father to their child. He said he didn't mind if it was a boy or a girl, but she knew he wanted a son. If it was a boy, he would teach him how to work with his hands, how to work with wood. If it was a girl she wondered if he could be persuaded to do the same.

Despite his practicality she sometimes thought of her husband as naïve. He had fixed ideas about things, like when he bought this house. They had argued. She understood that he wanted to live near where he worked, but she had advised against buying a house here. They should have bought a house somewhere that other people would want to live, that way its value would go up. They could either live there and he could drive further to the factory or they could rent it out and use that money to rent something cheaper near where he worked. But he thought that this was too complicated. It didn't make sense to him to own a house that someone else would live in while he lived in someone else's house. Besides, you never knew with tenants. They wouldn't look after a house as well as they would themselves. In the end she had let him have his way. Then the factory closed down and he was left with a house and no work, and payments to make to the bank. That was when he started driving the truck that took him away for days at a time, driving to logging camps, bringing the timber to ports where it would be exported overseas. It was a job, even if it didn't pay particularly well. But it also meant that she was stuck in this house on her own half the time, growing bigger every day. She spoke to the baby to fill the silence. If her mind was anxious about having her first child her body seemed to know what to do. She tried to stop worrying and scrolled on her phone looking for advice as to what to do and when. Asking the machine simple questions she had never really thought that much about. When did babies start to get their teeth, or stop drinking milk, or start to walk or talk? Though she found answers, they left her dissatisfied. She would learn them through experience in her own time.

The gaps between the lightning flashes and the thunder started to lengthen again. Though the rain still hammered on the roof she felt herself breathe more easily. The worst of the storm had passed. She wondered how long it would take for the electricity to come back, the internet, the phone. So strange being completely disconnected to the outside world. Water was seeping in under the door. A lot of water.

Half an hour later she was sitting with her husband, both of them cross-legged on the table, and the water still rising. They had dashed around trying to lift things off the floor, but apart from the shelves there was nowhere to put them. A small plastic stool she used in the bathroom floated in the water, knocking against the table as if asking for attention, wanting to be saved. The small amount of food there was in the refrigerator sat on the table between them. Their bed was already under dark muddy water. Their few clothes all ruined and submerged. She was so tired. She hadn't slept all night, but how to sleep at a time like this?

The cold water woke her. She must have dozed off leaning against her solid husband. Now the table was submerged. He had promised her that the water wouldn't get any higher, but he had no way of knowing, and the water evidently had different plans. First light was creeping into the sky. Her husband opened the door again, this time fighting against water instead of wind. She climbed down from the table and waded to the door. Outside was like a lake. Here and there were small islands made of the top halves of houses and the crowns of trees. The sun rose quickly. Soon it was hot as well as wet. It was no longer raining but the water still continued to rise. They drank from a plastic bottle and ate some slices of bread. There was no question of being able to cook anything. Besides, almost all the food was spoiled now in any case.

They waited an hour, two hours, three, waiting for the water to subside, sitting on chairs propped on top of the table, their heads almost touching the ceiling while their feet dangled in the water.

What they needed was a boat. That way they could make their way to somewhere dry, somewhere with food and clean water to drink. Her husband designed a raft in words, listing the things they had to hand, listing pros and cons. Eventually he settled on the door. Alone, it would float, but with their combined weight it would sink. They needed something to make it buoyant. She suggested the collection of empty plastic bottles they kept because they seemed too useful to throw away and which were now floating around them, drifting slowly, looking for a way out, clumsily bumping into walls. With some string her husband tied the bottles together, then unhooked the door from its hinges and attached the makeshift flotation devices. He tested it, sitting in the centre of the raft. It held his weight and floated but still wasn't buoyant enough to support them both. They had nothing they could use for paddles.

She took her husband's place and sat on the raft with one hand on her belly, whispering reassurances to the baby, to herself, while he pushed and steered the raft out of the house into the searing sunlight and through this altered shining waterscape. Sometimes he was just waist-deep. Sometimes the water rose up around his chest. Other times he held on to the back of the raft, the door, and kicked his legs. There didn't seem to be anyone in the neighbourhood. Perhaps people were trapped inside their homes. Or maybe they had left during the night when the water had first started to rise.

It was hard to tell where they were, any familiar landmarks erased. The houses all looked different, shortened, often with just the roof showing. She saw a monitor lizard lazily swim past, its head raised to take in the unexpected sight of a pregnant woman sitting on a floating door. Later a rat tried to climb aboard. She grabbed its wriggling wet body and flung it as far as she could throw. The rat landed with a splash, then altered course to swim towards a nearby tree instead.

The sun rose higher. Her skin burned. She was thirsty and tired and wet. Though he didn't complain, she knew her husband was exhausted.

Years later she would tell the child how, not long after she threw the rat, they saw the boat. The child always seized on this detail, as if there were some connection between the two, some chain of cause and effect linking rat to boat. If there had been no rat there would have been no boat. But for the mother there was no connection. It was just the sequence of events. Though her child's insistence to the contrary made the mother smile every time she told the story. Many years later yet it was the child, now fully grown, who smiled as the old woman told the story of the child's interpretation of the facts, the adult child picturing the child listening to the original story as someone else.

She heard it before she saw it, its engine thrumming as the

boat moved slowly in the distance. She shouted and waved. Her husband kicked harder, steering the door in the direction of the boat. The boat turned towards them. There were three men aboard. One manned the rudder. A grey-haired man sat in the stern, shading himself from the blazing sun with a large umbrella. The third man was holding something, some sort of camera. The camera turned towards them as she waved and called for help, then it turned back to the grey-haired man with the umbrella to catch him waving in reply. The cameraman lowered the camera. The boat turned and moved off into the distance.

The petrol station was underwater. They had hoped to find help there. People. Food. Something to drink. Their hopes were answered. Three dark-skinned young men sat on top of the awning that in a different distant drier world once shaded the petrol station forecourt. The men had some boxes with them. Seeing the couple, one of the men took something from a box and swam out to meet them. He handed them two bottles of water and a packet of biscuits. She had trouble deciphering the man's accent at first, but understood that the men had taken the food and water from the petrol station shop. They had been waiting all day for help to come, but had seen no one. The woman suggested waiting with the three young men, but her husband was wary. Despite being exhausted they would keep moving.

They came across a submerged house. Part of the roofing had been torn off in the storm, but the attic space was above the waterline. The husband climbed in to investigate. It would do as a shelter of sorts. He helped the woman climb off the door and then dragged the door in behind them. The space was small and narrow and hot, but it was dry and shaded. Evidently bats had used this space as a home. The smell of their droppings was overpowering at first, but she soon got used to it. Her husband arranged the door across the rafters and they sat on it together now, sharing the water and biscuits the foreign man from the petrol station had given them. After that they slept on the door, both exhausted and burned from the harsh sun.

When she woke up it was dark. Venus shone brightly in the patch of sky she could see through the gap in the roof. She had no idea what time it was by the clock, but she knew for certain that it was the time her child had decided to make its first appearance in the world. She begged the baby to wait just a little longer, just another day or two until they could find a better shelter. But the baby would not be dissuaded, neither by telepathy nor by prayer.

Her husband bit through the umbilical cord, severing the bloody cord that bound her to the baby. She lay spent on the door, the baby now reattached to her body, suckling at her breast.

Her husband rummaged through the attic space, eventually finding an old cardboard box with some clothes inside. The clothes were dry but musty. He used them to help his wife clean herself and the baby as best he could, then used the remainder of the clothes to line the cardboard box, making a makeshift crib.

The men from the petrol station must have watched and seen where the couple had gone. Maybe they had noticed the mother's swollen belly. Maybe they had heard the baby's first cries. They arrived with more biscuits and water, cans of soft drinks, packets of potato chips and peanuts, the three of them glistening wet in the starlight, silent before the baby in the cardboard box. The couple thanked them and the three men stayed a while, then left, slipping through the gap in the roof and back into the water.

As the sun rose she fed her hungry baby. Her husband wondered if the water level was starting to drop, or whether it was just wishful thinking. They hoped and half expected that the three men from the petrol station would return, but they didn't. Still the couple remembered them in their prayers as they licked their fingers clean after eating more of the snacks, keeping some aside in reserve, rationing the junk food in case no other help came. But less than two hours later help did come.

They left the door behind in the attic and climbed aboard a boat, other people who had been rescued shifting aside to make room for the woman and her baby, her husband squeezing in among the other men.

At the relief centre she waited for a doctor to come and examine the sleeping baby she cradled in her arms. Then she saw the three men who had fed them in the flood, the men who had sat in silent awe at the improbability of the tiny baby sleeping in a box of rags atop a door in an attic that reeked of bat droppings, in a storm-damaged house surrounded by unforgiving water. They were on a television screen, shackled, heads hanging, being pushed inside a police van. Then the camera cut to a politician, almost certainly the same grey-haired man she had seen sheltering under the umbrella on the boat, while her husband kicked and splashed in the water, while she sat aboard the door, yelling for help. The same politician, who had seen them and then turned away from them and their predicament was now railing against the three men from the petrol station, arrested as looters who had callously used the floods as an excuse to break into private property and steal anything they could lay their dirty foreign hands upon, an example of everything that was wrong with the country. Things would change if he was re-elected, he promised. The woman sighed at the snake-tongued politician sidestepping the obvious fact that he was already part of the venal government in power and could already make changes before elections instead of making promises that were just undisguised threats.

After a brief examination, the doctor announced that the baby was in good health, as was the mother, though the husband was running a fever and clearly exhausted and would need rest. She was tired too but somehow found the strength to rummage through the piles of donated clothes and chose something for her baby to wear, a blue one-piece outfit that was too big but that would cover the baby's nakedness. She found a clean cardboard box, that according to the writing on the side once contained Milo, lined it with someone's cast-off sarong and made another cardboard cradle for her baby's second night. Later, volunteers brought food. The couple ate hungrily, scooping up the rice with their fingers. They were given places to sleep, new foam mattresses still in their factory plastic wrapping brought in on the back of trucks by charity organisations. Despite the unfamiliar surroundings and the crowd of strangers it did not take the woman and her husband long to fall asleep. As they slept the baby lay silently awake, listening to the sound of a hundred people sleeping, listening to the crisp sound of its own breath.

The following day the camera crews and politicians arrived, photojournalists busy snapping photos. Word had gotten around about the newborn child, the miracle baby, the flood baby. The story would make good press. The politician from the boat, unerringly sensing any opportunity for a spin, was eager to be photographed with the child. Without asking, he lifted the sleeping infant from the Milo box and held the baby up for the cameras, smiling proudly, as if he had been singly responsible for rescuing this flood baby. He handed the child back to the mother and vigorously shook hands with the husband in front of flashing cameras, congratulating him on the birth of a beautiful baby boy. The woman found herself facing the intrusive shining eye of a television camera. A microphone was thrust in front of her face. She held up her baby, now rubbing its sleepy eyes with tiny fists, and informed viewers everywhere that, despite what the politician had claimed, her miracle flood baby was not a boy, she was a girl. Then she told several million television viewers about the door that became a raft, then became a bed, about the monitor lizard and the rat, about the politician who had left them floundering in the water, about the three men from the petrol station roof who had brought them gifts of food and water.

All across the country, people talked about this young woman who had been momentarily beamed into their homes, this woman whose testimony had been removed from further news reports by the national broadcaster, this woman who was the mother of the miracle flood baby, this woman now heralded as a national hero whose testimony spread all over social media, filling the spaces the politician couldn't control.

An online campaign was set up to find the magic door, which was finally reunited with its hinges. The politician's attempts at damage limitation weren't enough to win him a seat at the next election, but that didn't prevent him from being appointed to the board of a major GLC.

Meanwhile, the three men from the petrol station roof lingered for years in a detention centre. One died in the first wave of the pandemic. Another was brutally and regularly raped by prison guards, until one morning he was found hanging by the neck from a rope plaited from strips of an old t-shirt. The only survivor of the three helped bury both his friends. He has stopped counting days and has given up any hope for the future, cursing the day he decided to follow his dreams and seek a better life in this place. Even the threat of deportation has become a broken promise. But he still sometimes thinks about the little girl, the baby in the cardboard box, his last night of freedom, spent atop a petrol station awning roof, and Venus shining in the night sky, reflected in the floodwaters.

Honeymoon Suite

The afternoon Giovanni died Julia was enjoying the first few moments of precious solitude she'd had in weeks. Though she would spend much of the subsequent days and weeks alone, none compared to the moments when she eased herself into the rocky pool shaded by towering Dipterocarps, prehistoric trees from Gondwanda that grew on the little island in the tropics. The water wasn't deep, but much colder than she expected. A delicious shiver, near erotic, raced through her body, raising goose pimples on her slender arms, pushing tightened nipples against the thin polyester cloth of her bikini top. Currents rippling through the water distorted the light brown smoothness of her long bare legs. She breathed in the rainforest's thick yeasty air and leaned back with closed eyes, feet lifting from the rock, long black curls of hair writhing in a dark medusan halo around her head.

She gave herself to the gentle tug of the stream, drifting the short distance to the edge of the pool, incalculably more luxurious than the cyan-tiled infinity-pool back at the hotel. She righted herself, nose barely clear of the glassy surface. The water slipped away down an inclined expanse of smooth Cambrian granite towards the unseen waterfall, then through the wooded valley below and to the ocean where jet skis inscribed fading white arcs of wakes. She gazed out further still to where sky and sea joined seamlessly, the horizon lost in a humid grey-blue blur.

Between her and this view, an ugly barricade of concrete poles and steel cable cut across the water and the rock. She didn't need to know Malay to understand the red signboard with white letters was a warning. For a moment she felt a twinge of apprehension for Giovanni who, inspired by a troop of marauding macaques, had just minutes before set out to explore the rocky slope beyond the fence.

She pushed her head under the water, drowning any worries for her husband, then resurfacing swam the few lazy strokes it took to cross the pool where she floated once again, losing herself in the liquid play of sunlight reflected on the undersides of leaves.

FAMILY AND FRIENDS surrounded her during the days leading up to the wedding. So much planning and activity – the caterer, photographers, the cake, the bridesmaids' dresses, the chauffeured limousine still to be booked.

Her father had brought his old guitar to the wedding dinner. He sat on a stool in front of a microphone and faced the two hundred or so wedding guests.

"This song is for my precious princess," he said, fingerpicking the opening chords to *Julia* from the *White Album*. He stopped, leaning into the microphone.

"Some of you know I play this song to my Julia for her birthday every year. I have always said that she was named after my own mother Giuliana, but this is not true. When I first heard this song, when I was younger than my daughter is now, I thought it was so beautiful that I wanted to love someone called Julia just so I could sing this song to her. Thank you to my daughter for making that dream come true."

He sang with moist eyes and a quiver in his voice caused by a combination of stage fright, emotion and red wine. Emotions won out and he put down the guitar. With tears streaming down his face he stepped into his daughter's waiting arms.

JULIA WAS thankful the coroner's report had ruled out suicide. For one, she knew Giovanni would never take his own life, but also if the death certificate had said he had killed himself the priest would never allow him to be buried in the graveyard alongside his grandfather.

She never got to see the body, or to give him a last kiss. The coroner said it would be better if she remembered him as he was alive, rather than be haunted by the terrible memory of his broken remains. In her grief she agreed and a week later, back in Italy, the sealed casket was lowered into the ground. The dark rings under Julia's eyes matched her mood and mourning clothes as her fingers shredded damp tissue papers.

Afterwards she regretted the closed coffin. She should have insisted. She should have seen him with her own eyes. She knew and understood the reality of his death, but on another level she couldn't accept that someone could be so alive and then so suddenly, so casually disappear forever. During sleepless nights she convinced herself that the whole thing was a hoax, some kind of sick practical joke. Apart from a piece of paper and the coffin there was no real proof that her husband was really dead.

Giovanni's mother refused outright to visit after the funeral, her absence noticeable and accusatory. When they thought she was out of earshot she knew her friends and family eagerly discussed Giovanni's death. They fell silent when she came into the room, studiously examining their fingernails or coffee cups. No one was indiscreet enough to say anything directly, but she could read the doubts and suspicion in their eyes.

She sees Giovanni impatiently unwrap the wedding present from their friends. It was a box, large and heavy. They didn't know what to expect, certainly not the concrete blocks placed inside as a joke. Hidden between the blocks was a gilded envelope and inside bookings for a weeklong honeymoon on a tropical island.

They were so exhausted by the wedding that they slept most of the long international flight then staggered blearily through the glass and chrome airport for the short connecting flight to the island.

When they finally checked into their honeymoon suite at the Pulau Intan Hotel and Resort their bodies were confused by jetlag. They found themselves waking up late in the day, the sun already at its zenith, the sand too hot to walk on. The first two days were spent lazing by the hotel pool, taking sunset walks along the beach. The sun sank behind the nearby islands, painting the sky golden and yellowing the sails of the boats out on the waves.

On the second evening they stopped to watch a local family fishing at the beach. Two teenage boys trawled a net through the shallows while a toothless old woman shouted loudly from the shore. At first they thought the old woman was encouraging the boys, but as the net neared the shore they realised she was berating them for ineptly allowing the fish to escape.

Julia refused to use the air-conditioning in the hotel room. It went against her environmentalist convictions so they slept with the fan on, though it did little to cool them beneath the huge mosquito net that enveloped the bed.

Giovanni moved closer. Julia pushed him away.

"It's too hot," she moaned. "Your hands are too hot. I'm sweating already. Stay on your own side of the bed."

She placed a bolster pillow between them so he wouldn't roll over against her in his sleep and wrap himself around her the way he did in their apartment in Milan.

By the third evening they were rested and finally adjusted to being on a tropical island. Until then they had felt a strange sense of unreality, as if they were dreaming and would wake up back at home.

After a day of kayaking in the mangrove swamps Julia stripped off and stepped into the bathroom, taking her third cold shower of the day. She left Giovanni sitting on the bed transferring the photos of the kayak trip from his camera to his little laptop.

When she finished showering she found the air-conditioning unit buzzing and the room chilled to a refreshing twenty-four degrees and Giovanni lying naked on the bed, his firm intentions pointedly clear.

"Well, it's supposed to be a honeymoon, no?" he said, smiling.

She joined him on the bed.

They didn't take precautions. They had married to start a family.

"Imagine if one day we can tell our son that he was conceived on our honeymoon on a tropical island. How romantic."

"You mean our daughter," Julia replied in mock indignation.

"Whatever will be will be, but I think it will be a son. He will grow up to be as handsome as his father. Almost as handsome."

She ran her fingers through his chest hair. He was the hairiest man she had ever known. He needed to shave at least twice a day to appear clean shaven. He hadn't shaved since they had arrived and already had the beginnings of a thick beard.

"Scimmia mia," she purred. "My monkey-man."

THERE WERE real monkeys in the forest, surly macaques pulling rubbish from the bins along the concrete staircase to the waterfall, licking ice cream wrappers and crisp packets instead of adhering to their natural diet.

"Look," said Julia. "Your cousins."

"No. Your cousins. My cousins are much more handsome."

At over one hundred metres tall the waterfall was spectacular.

Local boys with tracksuit legs for swimsuits dared each other to leap off high rocks to splash into the pool below. Tourists sat around on the slabs of granite, some soaking up the sun, others keeping in the shade.

Julia waited while Giovanni took a few photos, then they continued further uphill, passing a line of wheezing tourists on the stairs.

"Last one to the top has to pay for dinner," teased Giovanni, already starting to run.

Julia caught up with him near the top of the stairs, sticking her tongue out as she bounced past. They were both fit. They spent much of their free time outdoors, hiking in the foothills of the Alps, or spending long-weekend breaks climbing rock faces in the Dolomites. A little staircase like this was no obstacle, but the humidity made them sweat.

It was their passion for mountains and for climbing that had brought them together. They met almost ten years earlier at the university climbing wall. Julia had forgotten to refill her magnesium bag. Without the white powder her hands were slippery on the grips. Giovanni had just finished climbing a tricky overhang when Julia approached him.

"You can take all you need," he said, long eyelashes framing his alert blue eyes, a playful smile on his delicate mouth. "But only if you let me buy you a drink afterwards."

In a café nearby they talked about climbing and about their studies. Giovanni had stopped studying geology and had taken up urban planning instead.

"The only work for geologists is in the oil industry. I don't have a car, just a bicycle. I want to be part of the solution, not part of the problem."

Julia was studying biology, and in the years since they first met completed her doctorate while working as a consultant in an environmental management agency. Living together allowed them to save the money they planned to use to renovate the old stone farmhouse on a piece of land in the countryside outside Milan, an inheritance from Giovanni's grandfather to his only grandson. There were fruit trees, and after generations of careful nurturing the soil was fertile, though the vegetable garden had become overgrown.

Julia spent hours working on the plans for the renovated house, choosing the most ecological materials she could find. They would install solar panels, both for electricity and hot water, and a small turbine to catch the winds that blew up and down the valley every spring and autumn.

The farm was legally hers now. But how could she ever live there without him? Everything they had planned was gone. Her whole future had been erased. A family. A new home. The silly arguments over whether to keep the old half-rotten oak tree, or knock it down to make an entrance for the car. It was all so inconsequential and distant, as if belonging to someone else's life. She could give the land to Giovanni's mother, but that would be like an admission of guilt. This farm in exchange for your son's life.

Over and over again she played the moment he ducked between the wires. His little wave and smile. She would have given her own life to save him if she could. She never had the chance. Never even knew that he was gone. She couldn't help imagining his last moments. She kept pushing it away, but she would wake up screaming, having dreamt that she was the one falling.

Sitting sweating on the edge of the bed in her parent's house, where she had grown up as a child, her breath subsided, though she still felt the free-falling tug of the dark and empty void of her dreams.

SHE SHIVERED IN THE WATER, struck by a moment of clarity and sudden realisation. She was pregnant. There was no doubt in her mind, just the recognition of a fact, the idea arriving fully formed.

She climbed out and lay down on the warm rock, letting the

heat radiate into her back and legs and arms and fell asleep to the gurgling flow of water with both hands placed on her abdomen.

She woke to the sound of voices. It took her a moment to remember where she was. A young Arab couple sat on the other side of the stream. The man wore sunglasses and a baseball cap, with a sleeveless t-shirt and loudly coloured board shorts. There was some sort of thick gold chain around his neck. His wife was completely sheathed in black. Only her heavily made-up eyes and her decoratively henna-painted hands were visible. Julia knew the intricate designs and curlicues were a sign that the couple were newlyweds. She guessed they were on their honeymoon as well.

She suddenly felt very exposed in her little bikini and she was sure that behind his dark sunglasses the Arab man's eyes were roaming over her lithe body. She used a sarong to shield herself and got dressed, her t-shirt redolent of her own sweat as she slipped it over her head. She slid the sarong down around her waist and tied it so that it made a skirt that hid her legs entirely.

The Arab man was taking photos with his phone, extending his arm so that his covered wife appeared in the shot beside him. There was some mumbled discussion as they examined the results on the screen. The man stood up and spoke to Julia.

"You will take photo of us," he said, more an order than a request, but Julia obliged, wading across a shallow part of the stream to take the phone from the man's outstretched hand.

Just as she was about to take the photo the woman whipped aside the black cloth covering her face and flashed Julia a big warm smile. By the time she handed back the phone the woman had covered her face again, but she had enough of a glimpse to notice that the woman was very beautiful. It seemed strange to hide such beauty. It was something Julia never really understood. She would have liked to know what the woman thought about Julia's bikini and all that it revealed, but didn't feel comfortable asking, especially with the woman's husband still ogling her, despite the fact that she was now more modestly dressed.

"My wife ask you are alone?" said the man.

"No, I'm waiting for my boyfriend. I mean my husband. He will be back soon. He is exploring."

The Arab man muttered something to his wife and Julia saw the woman's head dip in understanding.

Giovanni had been gone almost an hour. She felt a moment of annoyance, but then let it go. It was good for him to have some time on his own as well. The only time they had been apart all week was when they used the bathroom, and though she loved him dearly she wasn't the type of woman who needed or demanded her husband's constant attention.

She didn't want to be the type of wife who constantly nagged, but as the minutes passed she had to admit that she was starting to feel impatient. She walked along the dry rock, feeling the smooth granite alternatively warm and cool against the soles of her bare feet as she passed through pools of shade created by the trees.

She followed the water until she reached the point where two streams flowing from the forest met. A signboard announced a trail that led deeper into the forest. She took a few steps, surprised by the coolness of the shade and the soft sandiness of the soil. She would have liked to venture further, but didn't want Giovanni to worry if he came back and found she wasn't there.

She left the trail and re-emerged onto the granite, following the smooth expanse of rock downhill towards the ugly fence.

The rock dropped away too quickly to see anything down-stream. She called her husband's name, but there was no reply. He had probably found a little pool of his own and was letting the water soak the tropical heat from his body.

The Arab couple had left and she was all alone. The sun started to set, the shadows of the forest creeping out to shade the rock where she sat. A mosquito whined invisibly around her. She noticed that her ankles had already been bitten, but resisted scratching them, knowing that would only make the itching worse. Instead she turned her irritation to her husband and mentally rehearsed the scolding she would give him when he returned. She tried to soothe herself by watching the hypnotising eddies in the water until her impatience got the better of her. She walked to the edge of the fence and called Giovanni's name again. There was still no reply. Perhaps the sound of rushing water drowned her voice.

She paced up and down, half-heartedly examining the trees and plants, turning back to look at the fence every few steps. As a trained botanist she knew the names of almost everything that grew in her native Italy, but here she was at a loss. She recognised bamboo and thought the tree with the roots that hung down from its branches was either a strangler fig or a banyan tree, but apart from that she couldn't identify the shrubs with the little red flowers, nor any of the trees with their tall straight trunks and or those with their great big buttress roots. Neither did she know the name of the dark algae that grew on the rock wherever it was wet, nor did she know just how slippery that algae was, how it made it impossible to grip the smooth stone underneath, so slippery that no spiked crampons, or ice axe, nor magnesium powder would ever help.

Two men in red and grey camouflage uniforms appeared from the top of the steps. They walked slowly towards her, as if stalking a skittish animal, as if wary that they might frighten her away.

The men stopped and looked at one other, both nervously shifting from foot to foot. Even before either of them spoke Julia knew the terrible truth, something slipping inside her like the irrevocable flow of the water over the edge of the waterfall, the water gone, but still flowing, outwardly the same, but changed forever.

The doctor's tests confirmed the intuition that struck her as she floated in the forest pool. Though she didn't believe in reincarnation she couldn't help feeling that the realisation that she was pregnant came at the precise moment of Giovanni's death.

The priest just sadly smiled and shook his head when she tried to explain that it must be the same soul, the soul of the person she had chosen to share and build her life and future with.

Her parents stood beside her at the graveside. Her father would never sing Julia for her again. She wiped her eyes and blew her nose, pushing the half-used tissue up her sleeve to join the others she had forgotten she had hidden there.

As the clay rattled down onto the coffin she touched her belly. It was too early for the swelling to show through the black cotton of her mourning clothes. She hadn't decided what she would call the baby if it was a girl, but if it was a boy she already knew his name.

Lime Pickled

Hidden inside a small glass jar, in a back alley, lives a small family of illegal immigrants. They have never found the lid of the jar, so they sleep with their feet facing out to the world. If they could read the label on the outside it would tell them the jar once contained lime pickle. It's not that they can't read, but the script they are familiar with is almost never seen in this sweltering tropical oven of a city. Theirs uses different angles and makes different sounds, and despite having more than a passing familiarity with the works of the great novelists and poets of their erstwhile home country they now find themselves rendered to all intents and purposes illiterate. That said, it would come as no surprise to the family to learn the previous contents of the jar. The pungent odour that still haunts its interior is a constant reminder. Besides, in a half-starved frenzy, not long after they first arrived in the city, their hungry tongues had licked the jar clean of any encrusted pickle residue. After four days with no food, they were glad to stumble across the jar and its meagre sour contents, but it wasn't until they had finished every last oily scrap that they considered using the jar as a home. It had taken them that long to realise how very small they had become, and that this must be why they seemed invisible to the uncaring eyes of the passing strangers who inhabited this strange festering sweat-pool of a city.

The Nail

Cruel sun flashes rusting shimmerscales, hammering the hot roof of my hut. Boats pass, rocking the platform in their wake. The nail protruding from the wood. No one stops here anymore. They continue out to sea and disappear beyond horizon's line, though I see the green glow of their lights at night as they fish for squid. I squat in the narrow slice of oven shade, longing for the cool shadows that come when the sun slips behind the ridge. It all tastes the same place, the wide-eyed boiling mass of slithering, the platform of puckering mouths bunched in too close, the hot outcrop echoing the sun skywards. Unblinking, I ask the lengthening one. For the nail I rise. Wedge bodies writhe. Light flashes on the knife.

The only ones to hear the shouted echoes are the birds, silent water scanning kites and eagles, perching ridgeline trees, sweeping down to snatching gleam, talons tearing tender sky. Garuda fishing with his toes. Snatch, latch and catch. The wide-eyed surprise of fish suddenly airborne. The unblinking mass of shadow slips into painful heaven, filling the cracked blue. Garuda, lift me skywards. Hear me suddenly airborne above this rectangle within a rectangle of water framed by sun-bleached wood. Then the shadow of the shadow of the wriggling would stop.

Island slideshadows bring me back. I cook some rice. I net and gut a fish. I always kill them sunslides, slice the salty slivers and thread them on a line for tomorrow's sun to cook. Cook them hard and jaw. The rest goes in the pot. The fish tail end of rice.

They surface in the sheltered safety of the wooden planks, rising only for food, or late at night, slicing black moonlit water with their gulping mouths. I lie beside them, smoking cigarettes beneath the stars, eavesdropping watery stories told only for the nail.

On cruel pillowfists I wake. Hut stumble and flop onto the sweatfoam of my shelterbed. I dream about the nail. Metallic greyness tinged with orange rust. Tiny diagonal crosshatched ridges on its flattened head. He brings my drumming shouts back crosshatching wide-eyed rippling. Now I keep hammering, beating rust with painful fists. I don't want to stub my toe, I don't want to stub my toe, I don't want to, but I do. Tear the tender webbing in between my toes. Slip between the bones, stretch and snap the sinews, cut through to the heel. Gaping nightmouths suckling the black pumping of my blood.

I wake to echoed screams. There is only silence, my ragged breath, the gently lapping waves.

Was the wood too hard? Did the hammer slip waterwards from the carpenter's hand before his work was done? Knife's wooden grip grooved and gouged, I have nothing I can use. If I could, I would swim, pick a reassuring island rock. Just a small one. Feel the snug cupped roughness in my hand, if I could swim.

I feed the fish, fill the cracked blue bucket with brown pellets from a plastic sack. Come glittering the every now my frenzied fish. Feel the shadow of the nail. More sacks of time until the hammer shouts.

Black water comes alive. Night waves breaking on the rocks. A slithering silver mass slivering moonlight. Fish scanning stars like I the nail. The lights don't snag them here. I squat and tilt, tip in some feed, walk ten steps to my right. Squat and tip again. Fifteen steps, squat, tip, and stand. The glistening bodies writhe. I work the listening perimeter to within a metre of the nail, then turn and walk and work, stopping short again. Work like the hour hand of the sea and disappear beyond.

The bucket is empty. The fish sink back down into the net.

Separated from the nail by the rectangle of murky sea I net the fish and kill them on the first slap every time. Holden by the tail, head slammed against the wood, staring at the nail the fish lifeless in my hand. I hammer on, skin glittered with metallic moonlight scales. Hammering until only a wedge of pulpy flesh remains. I throw it in the water, feed it to the fish. It's all the same to them.

Tomorrow for the nail I will learn to swim. Or maybe I will drown, it's all the same to me. The water now a lapping clock, shortening hour hand. I am perimetered by many - Rock, Water, Wood and Sky, but it is the nail alone that holds me fast, the nail alone that holds me fast.

MCO

Manicure Control Order

It was one of MCOs, don't ask me which one - RMCO, FMCO, EMCO, CMCO, SEMCO[1] – who knew MCO got so many different flavours? So confusing. One day open, next day shut. This SOP, that SOP. Can travel, but cannot travel interstate. Cannot use front door, must use backdoor instead. Like that also can? Must wash hands for at least one minute, at least four minutes, must wash hands after washing hands. I tell you, those shops and factories selling soap are very happy, but maybe they are the only ones. Everybody else stuck at home being miserable, hoping phone credit does not run out, hoping battery does not run out, hoping patience does not run out.

Five of us live together in one small flat. We never spent so much time there. Usually we come back for sleeping only, but now all day every day indoors. We cleaned that place like never before. Sweeping cobwebs, scrubbing floors, shining windows, the whole place smelling like pine, like a whole forest of pine. At least that's what it says on the bottle of cleaning product. I never smelled pine in real life. None of us have.

It's like holiday, except nothing to do. A very boring holiday. We cannot go look-see at the shopping malls, walking in the cold air-con, imagining we are rich and live in some winter place, like some mat salleh country or wherever. We cannot even go lepak by the sea near Jerejak, sitting in the shade of some tree, giggling as we watch the Bangladeshi workers fishing on their day off, standing in the water in their underwear only, brown shiny bodies so full of muscles from hard work all the time, muscles bulging when they pull their fishing nets.

Last time we go to Gurney, or take a bus to Batu Ferringhi and walk on the hot sand or with our feet in the water. Sometimes we go makan in George Town, maybe street food on Lorong Baru, or just close by in one of the food courts. Our favourite one is Super Tanker. We are lucky. Our saloon lady boss gives us one day cuti every week. Most workers only get one day in one month. Still, even if Penang is a nice place, jalan-jalan lepak here and there is money going, not money coming, even if we try hard not to spend too much. We all send money home to our families. We all have responsibilities to make sure they have enough to eat, that our little sisters can go to school so that when they grow up they don't have to do the kind of work we have to do.

All our laundry is washed and clean and dry, maybe for the first time ever. The kitchen never so tidy, all the dishes done. We look around and it looks nice. Well, nicer anyway. There is nothing else to do except sleep and eat and be bored. We scroll and scroll and scroll and read news, then stop reading news because all the news is bad. We watch video clips, and that gives us an idea.

It all started with a video of hairdressers giving free haircuts to homeless people. I can tell you that video got one hundred thousand over likes and donno how many shares.

Our saloon is for hands, not hair, but since the saloon is closed during lockdown, we come up with a plan. Maybe we can make a video with our phones and get likes and shares as well. Who knows, maybe we can start new lives as social media celebrities or influencers.

We talk about what we will do when we are rich and famous. I want to see the world, travel everywhere. But now with all this virus spreading everywhere, even rich people cannot travel, which makes me think that even with so much money, being in lockdown is being in lockdown and not much fun for anyone, whether rich people, or people like us who have to work and work and work. But rich people will definitely be more comfortable and not have to worry so much, worried about getting fat and not worried about being hungry.

But now no one can work. Our whole building is full of people stuck at home all day, people bored like us, wanting something to do.

Most of the time the hands we see in the saloon are okay lah. Soft-skin shopgirl hands, office worker hands, bored tai-tai chubby finger hands and too many shiny rings. Not many men customers.

First, we think about homeless people, because of the haircutting video, but somehow, donno how, suddenly all the homeless disappear, who knows where. Anyway, we cannot really go out, except for essential things like shopping for food. Then we realise we don't need to look very far.

Our block of flats in Relau is full of migrant workers. Mostly men. They all work with their hands. Construction workers, restaurant workers, factory workers, assembly line workers, wet market workers ... MANual labourers, the same M.A.N. as MANicure.

Our long balcony got many flats. Same on every floor. Every day so many people walk past, going to work, coming home, shift workers sleeping on the same mattress, one in the daytime, one in the night-time. Last time was like that. But now no more coming and going. No more beep beep beep alarm clocks or donno what all wake-up music from smartphones at the same time every day.

Instead now everybody is at home, wearing masks or old t-shirts tied around their faces when they want to go out to the pasar. Now everyone cooks at home. Men coming home with heavy sacks of rice, big bags of dal. Some want to go and fish at night, but they are afraid the polis tangkap them. Even fishing cannot. Must keep social distance from water, must keep social distance from fish. SOP.

We make a little sign with a piece of cardboard:

MANicure
Best Hand Care
Free/Percuma

One of my roommates is good at drawing. She adds a picture of a hand. A man's hand. Hands are very hard to draw, but still it looks good.

At first only a few men want to come. We think maybe they think maybe manicure is not manly, even though got M.A.N. inside. But not long after, got one long line waiting on the balcony outside our door. And before you say anything, don't worry, we make them stand one metre apart. Must respect SOP, or else.

One of our neighbour boys got a big sheet of plastic and he and his friend put nails in the wall and tied a string so we can hang the plastic across our room, like a big curtain. We cut holes in the plastic, just big enough for one hand to fit. We want to make it nice, comfortable, with chairs, but we need ten chairs, five for us on one side, five for customers on the other side. But even with all our neighbours we cannot find enough chairs. We decide everyone can sit on the floor, like they always do anyway. Imagine landlords cannot even give one chair. We thought it was just our flat, but everyone else same same.

When the men come into our flat they for sure have to wear a mask and use sanitiser first. Everyone sits, five in a row, five in a row, us on one side, the men on the other side, facing on opposite sides of the big plastic. It is funny to see at first. Just these man shapes through the plastic and five hands sticking out.

You will be shocked to see some of those hands. Cuts, scars, hard skin, cracks filled with dirt that will never come out, blisters from hot oil, burns from turning roti canai. These are very different hands from the ones we usually see. The only ones with soft hands are the Nepali security guards. Everyone is jealous of them, standing in air-conditioning all day, nothing to do except watching pretty girls walk past.

"You see if you can tahan standing 12 hours with no sitting," said one Nepali boy when I teased him. "You sit all day. So lucky you. Every night my legs are paining me. Don't just anyhowly say."

People think manicure is just about cuticles and nail files and smelly chemicals like varnish and remover. But there is more than that. First, we use hand cream and massage the hand. But don't worry, there is no hanky panky or anything like that. Maybe this hand massage is the most important part. Everybody needs human contact, especially when they are far away from home, far away from family and friends. The M.A.N. in MANicure is the M.A.N in huMAN too. You can tell many of these men have never been touched by a woman for long time, maybe never, except by their mothers. Some of them are married and have children. Some of them have come to Malaysia so that they will have enough money to get married.

"No money, no honey," says one Pakistani man. "No wife, no life. I am saving all my money and all my love for the right woman. I will open a sundry dry-goods store and we will work there and live upstairs. My brother also he will do the same. We will share. He is currently in Dubai working. Maybe when my contract finished I am also going to Dubai."

After the hand massage we use nail clippers to cut the fingernails, but some of the men have chewed their nails so badly there is nothing left to cut.

"I can make more pretty with colour," jokes one of my housemates.

"Okay," says the man whose hand she holds.

"Really?"

"Yes, why not?"

Afterwards he shows his shiny painted nails to his friends. Now half the men also want coloured fingernails. It is more work, but also more fun and everyone laughs and laughs. Some keep laughing until they are crying. When you are far from home and missing everybody, laughing can very easily turn to crying. We all know this.

We never ask for money one, but some give anyway, one ringgit, two ringgit, much cheaper than lady-boss charges at our saloon, but by end of the week we have made ... well I won't say how much we made. None of your business lah. Some don't give money, but bring food instead – tapao fried noodle, fried rice, donno how many roti canai with little plastic bags of curry sauce. The wet market workers bring vegetables – carrot, cabbage, kangkung, taugeh, who knows what all else. We can open a stall at the pasar malam we got so many vegetables, except because of SOP pasar malam don't have.

Some of the Nepali boys invite us to their flat for traditional dal bhat, rice with dal and some few vegetables. We accept, but not because they have the softest hands, or not only because they have the softest hands. I have to say that in that one we week all received many many offers of marriage, promising us new lives in Pakistan, Nepal, India, Myanmar, Vietnam, Cambodia, Laos, Indonesia, Thailand. For my dreams of travel I can have a husband in every country.

"When you come to Nepal you will taste dal bhat. At home we eat this every day, breakfast, lunch, and dinner."

"Every day?"

"Yes."

I think eating the same thing every day might get boring. But then I think it is better to eat every day than not eat every day.

Some of the men are crying on the other side of the plastic. We can't see, but we hear them sniffing, see the shadow move as they lift their free hand to wipe their eyes. So many have lost their jobs and want only to go back home to their home country. But with lockdown, even if got money, they cannot go out of Malaysia.

We hear so many stories.

"My nana-nani sick, but hospital is too far to travel. Now I worry for my family, that they all will get sick also."

"I am trying to send money, but how to send? My wife and children need money to eat."

"My family for three years I have not seen. My contract next month finished and I already pay for air flight ticket to Kathmandu. Now airline is not providing refund."

In many flats people are eating just two meals a day. Then one meal a day. Then one meal every second day. Soon we are giving the food that some men bring us to the other men. We also just eat one maggi mee in the morning, then one more maggi mee at night. We drink lots of water in between to feel full and start feeling so tired. Now we don't want to do hand massage and manicure anymore. We take down the plastic and take down the cardboard sign.

In the end we didn't even make a video. All our social media celebrity dreams are gone, just like the dreams we once had when we first left home to make our fortunes in this country. We have worked so hard and for so long for what? To be poor and hungry still?

Some people, are saying there is free food. There are eggs and cooking oil and rice, collected by some people. Other people are cooking food at home and coming to our neighbourhood with their cars and giving food to anyone who needs it. We go, but we feel bad. We did not come here to beg. But we are hungry, so we go.

Some of the men will not go to take this food. They are too proud. Some of them are too afraid if they go out the polis will tangkap them and put them in lokap. They have been hungry before, they tell us. Hunger is like a family member, an uncle no one likes, who comes to visit for a while, but will sooner or later go. We know that this is true. They tell us that after three days hunger is not a problem anymore. There is no more growling stomach, no need to eat, no energy to do anything. We also know this is true. We have watched our mothers cut one egg into four pieces so that each child can have a piece to eat, and we eat, even when we know she has not cut a piece of egg for herself.

This is why we take the free food. We say thank you and hang our heads and eat every shameful grain of rice. We go back and ask to take some food for the men who will not come, but already there is not enough for everyone. We go back home again and take off our masks and scroll and scroll and scroll and cry, and hope and pray this lockdown will finish soon.

---

1. MCO - Movement Control Order
   RMCO - Recovery Movement Control Order
   EMCO - Emergency Movement Control Order
   CMCO - Conditional Movement Control Order
   SEMCO - Semi Enhanced Movement Control Order
   FMCO - Full Movement Control Order
   SOP - Standard Operating Procedure

Return Guest

It's not often that I'm at the reception desk, but three of the receptionists hadn't shown up for the morning shift. No phone call or anything. At this stage I'm no longer surprised, just annoyed. Missing staff is an ongoing problem, not just for the Pulau Intan Hotel and Resort, but for every hotel on the island. They turn up eventually, they always do, with excuses about having to attend a funeral, or a wedding, or a circumcision, or their cat being sick. In truth it's not that big a loss. Even when they're here half of them don't understand the difference between being at work and actually working. They stand around smoking by the staff entrance telling each other stories about mothers-in-law possessed by evil spirits or some such superstitious nonsense.

It turned out to be not all that busy, which was just as well, because I was making the receptionists nervous and generally getting in the way. It was an excuse to get out of the office more than anything else. I never went into hotel work to spend my days driving a computer. I enjoy the customer contact.

"You are leaving us Herr Holzmann?"

"Ja, but I will come back. The cold weather back home ..."

Günter is a return guest. Steel grey hair, small blue eyes, leathery skin, clean-shaven apart from a neat grey moustache. He comes for two weeks every year. Always stays in room 307. He's an early bird. First in the pool in the morning, first in the coffee shop for breakfast, peeling his croissants and sipping coffee with imprints of his swimming goggles embossed on his face.

"Anything from the minibar?"

"No, nothing from the minibar."

"You need a limo to the airport?"

"Not yet. I have a late flight, but I wish to leave my luggage until later. This will be my last chance in the beautiful rainforest. You will call me a taxi for the waterfall?"

"I'd rather call you Herr Holzmann, but we'll get a taxi for you if you want."

I should have offered him a late check-out so he could shower before his flight, but I only thought of that later, when it didn't matter anymore.

That evening the concierge called through. Old Günter hadn't shown up for his airport limo. His luggage was still in the store room. Not good. I asked the concierge to contact the taxi driver who had taken Günter to the forest. The concierge called back to say the driver had suggested waiting for Günter at the car park, leaving the meter running no doubt, but Günter had said he would find another taxi back. Maybe Günter had been running late and just went straight to the airport.

There are only three flights from the island in the evening, so I called the airport to check with the airlines. I got lucky on the first call. They had Günter's booking, but he hadn't checked in and the flight had left without him.

Room 307 was marked vacant/cleaned in the system, so I blocked it for the night and told reception to inform me as soon as Günter turned up.

In this profession you have to be a people person. The default mode is looking after the guests' well-being. There's also a certain paternal instinct that kicks in when you have almost 500 staff and 200 guests to look after. I couldn't help feeling worried for the old man. I started to imagine the worst. I called the hospital, but they had no one matching his description, just a handful of people suffering from jellyfish stings, a young woman who had broken her leg in a parasailing accident and a boy who was in a coma after being hit by a jet-ski.

It wouldn't be the first time tourists went missing in the forest. Once you leave the trail it's very hard to get your bearings. They usually reappear a day or two later, a little worse for wear, but the island isn't so big that you could stay lost forever, unless you slipped down a ravine, or twisted an ankle. And there are snakes of course. And scorpions. Even wild boar can be dangerous. Just thinking about it made my heart beat fast. I popped a bubble on the pack of valium I keep handy in my desk drawer. I thought about breaking it in half for about half a second, then washed it down with cold coffee from the bottom of my mug before calling the police.

The superintendent promised to organise a search party. They would set out at first light from the waterfall car park. It would be impossible to find anyone in the forest in the dark. That might be true, but probably it was more to do with the islanders being afraid of being in the forest at night and the spirits they say live there. I told the superintendent I would join the search party and drag along a few staff members too.

The following morning five of us from the hotel joined the police and the other volunteers. There were twenty of us altogether. One of the older men, a chap with a towel wrapped around his head, mumbled something. Arzul, the hotel's recreation manager, translated for me and explained that before we could go into the forest we had to ask the forest spirits' permission to enter and ask to be allowed to pass unharmed. Everyone bowed their heads in silence for a moment, so I did the same.

Climbing the concrete steps towards the waterfall set my heart going and circulated the heavy dose of caffeine I'd taken to counteract the effects of the previous night's valium. I struggled, but I managed to keep up with the other men.

It's easy to forget how beautiful this island really is. I don't go to the forest often enough, especially early in the morning. The soft sunlight made rainbows at the waterfall. But we weren't there for sightseeing. We spread out and looked around the giant boulders and between the trees. No trace of Günter.

More steps uphill. I'm a little out of shape. Even though it was cool beneath the trees I was sweating and panting by the time we reached the top. The superintendent asked me what Günter had been wearing when he left the hotel, but the only way I could picture him was in the black swim shorts he always wore while sunning himself by the pool. I didn't think it necessary to share that detail, so said I didn't remember.

There's a clearing where two streams come together, a confluence, I think it's called. Then it flows down over the edge of a precipice to become the waterfall. People die here every year. The local authorities have put up warning signs and a wire fence across the stream, but there are always adventurers who believe that they are immune from risk and cross the barrier to explore. Just a few months earlier one of our guests had died that way. A young Spaniard, no, an Italian on his honeymoon. Tragic story. There wasn't much we could do to comfort the wife, but I comped her hotel bill, though I suppose that was a small consolation.

I couldn't imagine Günter climbing past the barrier and the warning signs. There was a sign at the hotel pool that said that swimming was allowed from seven a.m. until ten at night. If Günter arrived even five minutes earlier he would wait until it was exactly seven before getting in for his morning swim. In any case if he had followed the same route as the unfortunate Italian we would have found his body already. I pushed away the image. I preferred to think of him as still alive.

We continued deeper into the forest, following a clear trail for about an hour. We split up into smaller groups. Some disappeared over a ridge and joined us a little further on. Wherever we could we spread out in a line on either side of the trail, but there were places too overgrown to pass. Some of the men slashed at the plants with parangs. It was obvious that Günter couldn't have pushed through the undergrowth, but they seemed to enjoy the show of manliness involved.

We kept slowly moving uphill until we reached the base of the mountains. At seven hundred metres they are not exactly the Alps, but they are steep. I had never ventured this far inside the forest, but the local men seemed to know their way about. Combined with the humidity and the rough landscape the going was quite tough. I kept wondering if old Günter could have made it this far, but then reminded myself that even if he had at least twenty years on me, with all his exercise he was probably far fitter than I was.

It took us a few more hours to reach the summit. Apart from plastic bags, empty mineral water bottles and cigarette butts there was nothing there. The view was almost worth the climb. Many of the surrounding islands in the archipelago were visible and I could just about make out the smear of the mainland on the horizon. Sometimes it's easy to forget you are on an island, but being able to look from coast to coast really brings it home.

Some of the men were smoking in little groups and laughing among themselves, like youngsters on a school outing. Then the old man with the towel tied to his head said something and the rest fell quiet, mumbling in their indecipherable dialect. I asked the recreation manager what they were talking about.

"They say that the German has been taken by the spirits of the forest."

By the time we got back to the carpark it was almost dark. I rode with the police to the station, answered a few questions, filled in some paperwork.

"There's not much more we can do," said the superintendent. "If he is lost and injured he might never find his way out of the forest. But maybe he is not there. Maybe he is somewhere else. We are asking all taxi drivers if they see him."

I had heard Günter tell me himself that he was going to the forest, so I felt sure that's where he was, but at least the policeman wasn't subscribing to the 'taken-by-the-fairies' theory.

That was Wednesday. Günter had been missing since Tuesday.

On Friday I got a call from the front desk. Günter had returned.

"You came back, Herr Holzmann," I said on reaching the reception desk. "We are very relieved to see you. Are you alright?"

"Yes, I am fine thank you, and you?"

"But where have you been?"

"I told you this morning. I have been in the forest. Now I must go to the airport to catch my flight."

"The airport? But you missed your flight, Herr Holzmann. It left four days ago."

"You have a strange sense of humour. Now really I must get my luggage and go or I will be late."

I started to wonder if the old man was suffering from Alzheimer's.

"Do you know what day it is?"

"Yes, it is Tuesday."

"Today is Friday, Herr Holzmann. You left the hotel on Tuesday. We've been looking for you ever since."

"Nonsense. Please be serious. I need to catch this flight or I will not make my connection."

"I'll get the porter to bring your luggage. Why don't we sit for a moment?"

I led him over to a sofa in the lobby, picked a newspaper and showed him the date.

"We had a search party looking for you in the forest Herr Holzmann. I even went myself. You have been missing for three days."

"No, this is not possible."

"Well, how do you explain the date on the newspaper?"

"The printer obviously made some mistake."

I picked up a different newspaper and handed it to him.

"I do not understand," he said, doubt creeping into his voice.

"Tell me everything you remember after you left the hotel," I said, thinking that if he mentally retraced his steps he might remember where he had been.

"I took a taxi from here. I walked up the steps. I went into the forest, stayed there for some hours, then came back down the steps and took a taxi here."

"Let me get you something to drink. Tea? Juice? Something stronger? It's on the house."

I used the excuse to check with the concierge. I knew he logged every taxi that brought guests to the hotel. The island being small, and everyone being related to one another, he quickly found the taxi's phone number and gave him a call. The taxi driver confirmed picking Günter up at the waterfall car park about an hour earlier.

"Tea will be along in a moment," I said, settling back down on the sofa opposite Günter. "Did you enjoy yourself in the forest? See any animals? Monkeys?"

"Ah yes, monkeys there are many, but they never go near the village. The people there have taught them not to steal their fruit. I would not have thought this possible."

"The village?"

"Yes, the village."

This wasn't the first time I had heard stories about a village in the forest, but everyone knew that it was just that – stories of a place that didn't really exist, stories to tell while hanging around at the staff entrance smoking cigarettes.

"I've never visited the village. Where is it exactly?"

"It is difficult to find, but I met a man on the trail who brought me there. It really is a lovely place. The women were cooking. They invited me to join them for food. Very friendly people. They live very simple, but have so many fruit trees and so many fruits - rambutan, and durian, and mangosteen, and mangoes and papaya. Very fresh. Straight from the trees."

"Rambutan this early in the year? Usually, the season is in four months' time."

"Oh yes, very sweet and ripe. And also meat and rice prepared with wild herbs from the forest. Very good. Your chef could put them on the menu."

Nothing in Günter's manner told me that he was suffering from memory loss, or telling anything but the truth. He accepted the fact that he had missed his flight, though he had no explanation. He stayed in room 307 for another night. The airline agreed to change his ticket and he was able to fly out the following evening.

I was so relieved to see him that I didn't remark straight away, but there were details that bothered me beyond his story. Apart from the fact that the village doesn't exist, anyone having spent three days and nights in the forest could be expected to look dishevelled and dehydrated. The mosquitoes would have ravaged his skin. But he looked healthier and happier than I had ever seen him. At the very least he should have had the beginnings of a beard, but apart from his neat steel-grey moustache, he was perfectly clean-shaven.

Mutiny in Kampung Merokok

It should have been a peaceful day in Kampung Merokok. At least that was what I pictured when I set about writing what was to be a simple and straightforward story featuring an amiable cast of nicotine-fuelled characters that would unquestioningly comply with my puppeteering. But one by one as they appeared it became clear they were drawn from defective stock. Rebellious and recalcitrant, they resisted my deific whims with a strength of conviction that in other circumstances might be considered admirable, unanimously refusing to adhere to the plotlines I had so carefully devised. Nor would they parrot the simple lines I had prepared for them to utter between thoughtful drags on their cigarettes.

Aisha, the teacher's pet, presumed to be timid and obedient, kicked off the fuss by creating a scene during the morning school assembly, tearing off her tudung with a scream. As if that wasn't enough she hitched up the long skirt of her kebaya, squatted and defecated there and then in the playground. I was as shocked as anyone, perhaps more so, as none of the other characters present seemed particularly surprised by her behaviour, and when I questioned her apparent lack of underwear I was summarily informed that many of her schoolmates regularly went commando and that

I was obviously out of touch with the realities of teenage school-goers to focus on such an insignificant detail.

Meanwhile, Puan Hamizah changed her mind about quietly savouring the steaming mug of Milo I had prepared her. She turned off the television, forgoing her usual daytime regime of Indonesian and Korean soap operas, and went directly to the neighbours' house with the firm intention to berkhalwat with Fahmi, a young man ten years her junior and her best friend's son.

Fahmi, generally averse to idle gossip, either as a subject or a practice, liked to keep to himself. Like most of the population of Kampung Merokok, even if he invested more time, effort, and money in smoking than he did in prayer, he still considered himself religious. But lately he found his mind increasingly troubled by the graphic and gruesome images featured on the cigarette packs, bringing to the subject the obsessive attention to patterns that often heralds certain forms of mental illness. He had been drawing dead babies all week. He assumed the babies were dead. They didn't look too good in any case, which he understood was the point. But a simple photo wasn't going to make him, or any of the other denizens of Kampung Merokok, swear off smoking, quite the contrary, in fact. If anything the images, which included gangrenous feet, cancer-riddled throats, blackened tar-clogged lungs, and rotted gums and teeth, reinforced the inherent ugliness of life. If depictions of pain and suffering underlined the inherent fragility of life, by being banalised and made quotidian, they lost their power to shock. If life was so shit, reasoned Fahmi, it may as well be over sooner. He lit another stick, consoling himself that he was taking control of his destiny by committing slow suicide by smoking. Still, this business with the babies had him spooked. Seventeen in a row this week and it was only Wednesday. There was a message there, he was sure, though quite what it might be he had yet to decipher. When Puan Hamizah knocked on the door it came as a welcome release and distraction from all this excessive cogitation and he forsook his cigarettes, allowing one to smoulder in the ashtray while he assiduously made himself a more than willing accomplice to his neighbour's adulterous plans.

None of this was featured in my initial outline so I decided to leave these two characters to their debauchery and turn my attention to the local policeman. I had initially tasked him with arresting Rafiz Zaharuddin for trafficking syabu, but now it transpired that he was refusing to hold Rafiz in his cell, insisting between puffs of suspiciously scented hand-rolled cigarettes that to do so would be an injustice and persecuting such an enterprising young fellow for simply trying to make a quick ringgit was just plain wrong.

To crown it all off the Imam, an inveterate chain-smoker and as pious a man as his calling ever befitted, and noted for his punctuality, gave in to sloth, lazing in the comfort of his bed well past the usual hour, failing to make the morning call to prayer, the result being that those who had not yet risen slept late, throwing the day's activities out of alignment at its very inception.

Unbeknownst to me, an angry mob of villagers had been secretly holding meetings. They assembled en-masse baring teeth, bearing cangkuls and newly sharpened parangs, and turned themselves against me, insisting, while smoking furiously, that if I didn't immediately construct luxury villas and furnish them with expensive cars they would riot.

Outnumbered by this unruly and mutinous cast I had to concede defeat. Loathed though I was to do so, I finally abandoned the manuscript, and the story of Kampung Merokok remains unwritten to this day, which all considered, is probably for the best.

You Drive

You don't own the taxi cab. You rent it by the day. It takes at least four fares to cover petrol costs. Maybe more. Petrol prices going up. It's hard to make a living. It's hard for everyone. Crime is going up. Everything is going up these days. Except the rain. You like the rain. It's good for business. No one wants to walk. When it rains you use the meter, banking on the guarantee of traffic jams.

You drive. Your hands hold the wheel. Your foot moves from brake to gas to brake. You know that it is you driving, but it seems like someone else. Or something else. Something as automatic as the transmission of the car. You don't need to think. Your hands and feet think for themselves. They have become part of the machine. The boundaries blur. Where do you stop? Where does the car start? It's no longer clear. You know these streets. They are burned into your brain. Imprinted so deeply that you no longer have to think. Your mind wanders free. The car drives itself. The car and the parts of you that belong to the car. The car and the parts of you that belong to the city streets.

You arrive at your destination without knowing how you got there. But it is not your destination. It is always someone else's destination. You keep driving without getting any closer to where you want to be. At home. With a wife. With a family. At home. In your own country. With your own people. With your own friends. At home does not exist. You wonder if you will ever reach that destination. Your destination. If you drive far enough and long enough you hope someday you will. But your destination is not getting closer. It gets further every day. It recedes into the past. Like blurred reflections in a motor-shaken rearview mirror. Through a rain-smudged rear window. You only glance back occasionally. Your destination is behind you now. If you keep driving maybe you can go full circle on the ring road and reach it from the other side. Years spent behind the wheel. Years that sun-bleach memories. They fade. The details getting lost. All you see now are just the outlines. Even some of them are blurred.

Every day you save a little bit. Your savings start to grow. You are getting closer now. The memories flood back. They grow sharper. The colour returns. Vivid scenes of childhood fields. The smells of woodsmoke and cooked rice. Glimpses of smooth brown skin. Flawless skin so fresh and new. Skin that hasn't lost its elasticity. You see eyelashes. Long and curved. You see an innocence you know you've lost. It's almost too much to bear. So you drink it all away. You waste your money on the women who rent their bodies by the hour. And now you are back closer to where you started from. Before you started getting closer to going back.

The past and future fade. Now it is just you. You. You in this car. You. In this city. You. And the rain pouring down outside.

He raises a hand. He has seen you. He knows you have seen him. He is tall. Long. You remember this. His black coat is long. It reaches past his knees. His face is long. His nose is long. His chin tapers down into a pointed beard. Despite the rain he wears dark sunglasses. You know that he is not from here. You flick the indicator. You pull in off the road. He has a suitcase. You pop the lock release for behind. You are about to step outside to stow his luggage but he has already done it himself. He is beside you. You don't like that. You prefer it when they sit behind you. Each one to their own place. The front of the car is yours. Now he's filling half that space. Filling half your space. His aftershave is strong. Santalwood perfume. You quite like the smell. He doesn't talk. Some of them don't. Some of them never shut their mouths. You relax. You drive. Your hands and feet drive the car.

The santal reminds you of the temple. Images of coconuts and flower garlands. Marigolds and jasmine. Brightly painted gods. Jai Lakshmi. She smiles indulgently from her pink lotus-blossom throne. She has always been there. Forever in your life. Again you are back home. Running barefooted through the fields. You reach the destination. His destination. He doesn't argue about the fare. Some of them do. Some of them never want to pay. He is barely out of the car when an auntie slides into the back seat. You see him in the rearview mirror. He is talking to two men. Then all three quickly walk away. The auntie wants to talk. You talk. You reach the destination. Her destination. You drive and find another fare. He leans into the open door. The airport. You nod and smile. You will earn some money today. Jai Lakshmi. The rain has stopped. You step out to help him with his luggage. The space is already full. The long man's suitcase. He left it behind. You remember you forgot. Your mind drifted away. Whisked away to childhood on wisps of his perfume. Only your hands and feet were left behind. You have to return the suitcase. But now you have a fare. You try to remember the destination. His destination. All he said was please stop here. Even though you were only hands and feet you find a recording in your mind. Details etched on your brain-burned map. You can find the place again. But can you find the man? It bothers you all the one-hour drive to the airport. You know your fare is talking. You can hear but you don't listen to a word. You say uhuh and mmm and nod from time to time. Your mouth knows how to do this without getting your mind involved.

The queue at the airport taxi rank is long. You need a return fare. You get a coupon from the pre-paid taxi booth. By the time you reach the city, it is dark.

The suitcase weighs heavy on your mind. You return to the drop-off point. You need to find the long dark man somewhere in the neon-sparkled night. There is no hotel. No hint where he might have gone. You drink tea and ask your fellow countrymen. Have you seen a long dark man? But he is gone. No one else has seen him. You will never find him now. Perhaps there is a clue in his belongings. You can look inside the case. You want to be away from prying eyes. You don't want to be mistaken for a thief. Your feet and hands drive you to a darkened lane. Headlights pick out the eyes of rats and cats. No one is around.

The suitcase weighs heavy in your hands. It has a lock. A combination of three numbers. A thousand possibilities. Like the sahasranama. The thousand names of God. This could take all night. You have all night. You pick the most auspicious number. *One oh eight*. The suitcase opens at first try.

You are in shock. Your hands are shaking. Your knees are weak. There is no address. No dirty laundry. No neatly folded shirts. There is only one thing inside the case. Money. More than you have ever seen. Bundles of American dollars. Twenties and one hundreds. It could take all night to count them. You have all night. Quick calculations tell you there are millions. You need to return the money. You need to find the long dark man. Again you drive around the neighbourhood looking for a clue. Your hands and feet no longer drive. You have to tell them what to do. What to do? You wish someone would tell you what to do. So much money. More than you could ever spend. You can keep it. You could buy anything. You can buy this car. But you don't need this car. You never have to work again in your whole life. There is nothing you cannot do. The future becomes the present. You can have anything you want. What do you want? You don't want to be a thief. You are not a thief. You want to return the money. You can't return the money. You can leave the country. You can go back home. You can have a wife. A child. A child running barefooted through the fields. Your fields. The child doesn't need to be barefooted. It can wear the best shoes. You cannot keep this money. It is not yours to keep. You did not earn it. You can give it all away. It is not yours to give away. You can keep it and no one will ever know. You did not steal the money. There hasn't been a crime. There will be no punishment. It is yours to keep. Lakshmi smiles indulgently. Goddess of abundance. Goddess of wealth. An endless stream of golden coins pouring from her open palm. This is the repayment for devotion. She pays you back for each time you believed. You are free now. You have reached your destination. The destination is a starting point.

Your feet and hands have taken the car back under control. Or does the car control your hands and feet? The car follows its own brain-burned map. It brings you here. You park. You get out of the car. You carry the case up the steps. The bright lights blind your eyes. Someone talks to you. They talk to you. Your mouth doesn't know what to say. Your hands lift the case up on a counter. *One oh eight*. The men in uniform all gasp. They take you to a back room. They question you. They keep the case. They don't believe your answers. You say why else would I come? They shout at you. They push you. Then the beating starts. They kick you out the door. No one will believe you. You are bleeding. Your head is bleeding. Your hands are shaking. Your legs limp back to the car. You sit inside the car. Later your hand turns the key. Your feet push pedals. Your hands just steer. You drive.

The Green Fuse

The force that through the green fuse drives the flower
Drives my green age; that blasts the roots of trees
Is my destroyer. —Dylan Thomas

Twenty-seven holes, each approximately two feet deep and wide, were dug by a team of municipal workers, eager to be finished before the full heat of the day, but not enthusiastic enough to make an early start. They each took turns with the shovel while the others watched on, either panting or smoking cigarettes. I supervised from a distance. When night fell I brought a black plastic bag that contained various items that I carefully buried at the bottom of each hole.

A marching band of policemen, sweat stains ringing the armpits of their uniforms, competed with music blaring from loudspeakers tied to the shade trees that lined the road. From every lamppost, the Supreme Leader looked down at the crowds. Their shining faces reflected the searing sun. At first glance his face appeared avuncular, but on closer inspection it became clear that this was not the type of uncle you would trust with your children, a face as unsettling as a circus clown, simultaneously anodyne and terrifying. His smile was equal parts indulgent, obsequious, and condescending, with lips much too luscious and feminine for a politician, more suited to a prostitute, though of course, both occupations overlap, and which is the more noble profession is open to debate. His weak chin was supported by a flabby double, and spoke of a man ignorant of the meaning of moderation, while his cold omniscient and omnipresent eyes held all the calculating kindness and empathy of a murderer.

The ruling party's flag, a green kangkung leaf emblazoned on a white background, hung limply, weighed down by the hot and heavy air. Schoolchildren in blue and white uniforms, excited to be excused from school for the day, made up for the flag's torpidity by waving their own smaller flags, distributed earlier on the party's behalf by their teachers. All civil servants engaged in non-essential work, of which there were a great many, were given the day off, on the condition, of course, that they attended the inauguration of the park. Some were glad for the change of routine, others bemoaned the lack of air-conditioning.

Then there were the ordinary people: the fishermen and farmers and their families. Most had travelled from the villages on buses provided by the party. Some of the lucky ones received free t-shirts bearing the party's kangkung logo. Perhaps a few had come out of simple curiosity, a trait never to be underestimated, but most came for the promised bag of rice - a kilo per person, young or old. They brought babies, hooked on hips, or slung on their backs in sarongs. They brought the old and toothless, with sun-leathered faces and backs bent crooked from years of housebound squatting. They brought their misshapen children, who couldn't go to school, poisoned before birth by the toxic runoff from mine tailings that flowed into the streams and rivers.

They all gathered in the new park that was about to be dedicated to the party and its leaders as a symbol of the party's munificence. They loudly chatted, or quietly gossiped, sitting on the grass mats they had spread in every pocket of shade.

Some brought picnics of rice and cooked fish wrapped in banana leaves, sticks of satay meat dipped in peanut sauce, or shiny tiffin cans with curried meat and vegetables, while others gorged themselves on Kepsi fried chicken bought at the local outlet. They ate with their hands, licked their fingers, and waited.

The children grew restless. Babies, tired and overheated, loudly mewled. The band members, having laid down their instruments, drank brightly-coloured iced drinks bought from a nearby stall. Some of the civil servants left, making excuses no one believed, but most were too scared to go, knowing that their absence and lack of loyalty to the party would be noted.

Two hours later than announced, with a posse of motorcycle outriders heralding their arrival, the distinguished guests finally climbed from their limousines: party cadres, government ministers, members of the local royalty, almost all of them men, were hit by the wall of wet heat as they left the air-conditioned comfort of their cars. Some were visibly drunk and needed to be supported by their assistants, others waved cheerily to the locals. A few even dared shake hands with the flag-waving children, whose eyes were already turned upwards toward the helicopter that carried the Supreme Leader himself, and his latest diminutive wife, this one at least twenty years his junior.

SOME CALL ME A BOTANIST, others a bomoh, straddling the worlds of the seen and the unseen. I think of myself as a gardener, harnessing and gently guiding the forces of nature. Secrets have been passed down the matrilineal line of my family for as long, and longer, than can be remembered, secrets involving trees and the spirits of our forests.

Even as a young man, the Supreme Leader understood the symbolism of tree planting. I worked at the botanical garden and he turned to me for advice. I used all my charms, feminine and otherwise, to ensure it stayed that way. There is much that can be cultivated on the borders of botany.

"You don't look like secret service," said the hotel manager, handing me a master key and a list of the delegates' rooms.

"That's the point," I replied. "Are they all seated?"

"Yes, the first course has just been served. This size should fit you."

I took the ugly housekeeping uniform, and back in my room contemplated the woman in the mirror. She could pass for a member of staff — forties, a victim of time and gravity, slightly heavyset and over-ripe. A pair of thick-framed transparent glasses and a headscarf completed my disguise. I went from room to room, using the list the manager had printed out: Minister of Finance, Minister of Justice, Attorney General, Home Minister, and many others, all safely seated downstairs at a banquet in one of the hotel's luxurious function rooms.

"Housekeeping," I called, just in case. It wasn't unknown for our ministers to smuggle unofficial 'guests' to their rooms, but apparently all the delegates were behaving themselves this time, so far at least, which was a little disappointing. Such knowledge could have been useful as future leverage.

In each room I searched for a small personal object, a worn sock, a necktie, an undershirt, a toothbrush, anything they had used or worn, and preferably small enough that I could slip into the black polythene bag I carried. I made a note of what I had taken against the list.

Back in my room I shed the uniform and still had time to apply lipstick and eyeliner before going downstairs to deliver my after-dinner speech. I felt a smug sense of satisfaction knowing they were completely unaware of how the trees, whose Latin names I casually dropped, would be instrumental in shaping their personal and political destinies.

I had my own agenda in the type of trees I chose, but made flattering comparisons wherever appropriate or possible. Though it was politically sensitive to choose durian, the king of fruit, for the Supreme Leader, particularly with members of royalty present, whose power he was eager to usurp, I had backed him throughout his long career and was known for my unflinching, and admittedly opportunistic, loyalty. For the vice-leader I chose rambutan — a nondescript tree named for the soft hair-like bristles that grow on its testicular globes, but reliable for its seasonal sweetness. The Home Minister would plant a jackfruit tree, cousin of the durian, fast growing and long-lived, but taking several years to fruit. Jati, also known as teak, a slow-growing hardwood, with solid and durable timber, represented an investment in the future and seemed apt for the Minister for Industry. For the Minister of Communications I chose frangipani, which gives sweet-smelling flowers, but is essentially merely decorative, its main qualities being that it is easily cloned and its sweet perfume can mask unpleasant smells.

The following morning the workers returned with a lorry full of saplings and I made sure each tree was placed beside the correct hole. A red-faced shy young woman from the town hall followed us, tying wide red ribbons into bows around the slender trunks.

Everything went according to plan. The trees were planted, hands were shaken, speeches were made. Notes were taken and compiled into press releases, which would be featured heavily, along with official photographs and video footage, in all of the party-controlled media.

FOR MANY YEARS I tended the park and its trees, nudging and coaxing nature towards something harmonious and balanced. Sometimes drastic action was needed. Though the Home Minister's jackfruit tree was meant to thrive it was doing a little too well. He became arrogant and started overreaching the limits of his authority. I waited for the full moon, when the rising sap quickens, and lopped off the longest branches with swift swipes of my parang.

The Vice Leader, living up to his name, developed a penchant for underage girls and often beat them while under the influence of strong narcotics. The rambutan fruit on his tree was pinkish-red and hairy. I gripped them firmly, and with an emasculating cut-throat razor sliced them from their stems.

Others were kept in line with occasional pruning. I nurtured them with compost and made sure they had enough water during the dry seasons. I allowed most of the trees to fruit, though I treated the roots of some with salt and watched them slowly wither, or dripped sugar water on their branches and let the ants and termites come. Occasionally I made incisions in the bark and watched the sap or creamy latex flow.

The park flourished and the country along with it, but a garden needs constant attention. There is no fallow winter season in the tropics where frost sterilises the soil and the gardener may rest; there is just the thrum of nature seeking constant expression in all its variations.

MEANWHILE, hundreds of kilometres away, a tract of protected virgin rainforest was illegally logged for its precious timber. Bulldozers removed the roots and the remaining vegetation was burned off to make room for a new palm oil plantation. I was connected to that forest and its trees in many ways and their plight became my plight. My health started to fail. I could no longer look after the park and its trees.

Only untouched forest remains in a state of true equilibrium, but when humans interfere with the perfect balance of nature, and then neglect it, we create an impenetrable hostile jungle. At first the weeds and grass came and untended grew knee-high. Thorny bushes popped up almost overnight. Within a few short years the garden was as if it had never been. Though the trees were still there, they were smothered by the undergrowth and overgrowth. Their fruits fell and were eaten by wild things or left to quickly rot, further fertilising the soil for the invasive plants and parasites.

Vines wound their tendrils around the branches and expanded their domain with frightening virulence, as if making up for time lost, as the creepers of corruption and religious fundamentalism spread their stranglehold through the country.

The Supreme Leader's face, hardened by the years, disappeared from the billboards and official portraits. Our new Supreme Leader, seeking supremacy in his supremeness, engaged another gardener of his own, a man instructed to tend the smothering vines and guide their strangling tendrils to create a shield that hides the fruit, so the Supreme Leader can keep them for himself and his ruthless cohort of chosen followers. But the laws of nature insist that all that grows must inevitably decay.

Island Time

People say there are only two speeds on the island:

Slow, and very slow.

But those who know the island well know that this is not true.

There is only very slow, and stop.

Seed

Weeks of currents, aquatic and magnetic, brought Penyu here again. She surfed the moonlit high tide waves, front fins tucked, and glided up onto the beach. The soft sand made her progress slow and inelegant. She began to dig. Soft-shelled eggs slowly filled the nest, fertilised by the seed of several fathers, nature hedging its bets that the strongest and fittest would continue the race whose only finishing post was survival. Still working in the dark she covered the glistening eggs with sand, then, as generations had done before her, for more than one hundred million years, returned into the sea.

The man shivered. The sea of stars had shifted. The waves still washed up on the shore, but now there was a band of smooth wet sand where the water had receded. Had Penyu been and gone, or was she yet to come? He had waited almost a year for her return, or any of her sisters or aunts and their precious cargo. Eleven months spent craving something other than rice and fish and tapioca. He stretched and waited until the stars began to fade.

He walked the length of the beach looking for tracks until he found Penyu's nest. He crouched, then slowly excavated the soft-shelled eggs, piling them onto the batik sarong he had brought with him. There were almost two hundred eggs though he couldn't count that high. Like most islanders he had little use for numbers any greater than half a dozen.

He thought he heard voices behind the hiss and wash of the waves breathing in and out upon the shore. They were faint at first, perhaps imaginary, but when he looked around he saw the boat. It was bigger than any vessel on the island and had more than a dozen men aboard. He raked his fingers through the sand, searching for any remaining eggs, then bundled up the laden sarong and withdrew into the shelter of the trees and undergrowth that marked the edge of the forest.

The boat drew closer. The men spoke an unfamiliar dialect, but he could understand most of what they said. Anchoring the boat beyond the breaking waves they half-swam half-waded ashore. Some carried their clothes in bundles held over their heads. Others brought baskets of firm-bodied gleaming fish. He watched them dress and gather firewood and soon the smell of cooking fish reminded him that he had not eaten in many hours. He hid the bundle of eggs in the undergrowth then ventured forth onto the sand, but from far enough away that the men could see him coming. Far enough away that he could escape into the forest if they seemed hostile.

He walked slowly back from the village, along the trail beside the rice paddies, carrying Penyu's eggs and a small package made of folded banana leaves. His reluctant steps stirred the dust that coated his bare feet and clung to the hem of his threadbare sarong. Wrapped inside the leaves were four silvery fish. A stranger had given them to him. He didn't know how to act around strangers. He didn't know how to refuse. Their lidless eyes had been clear, the sheen of their scales reflected the afternoon light, they smelled of the vast ocean beyond the island. He took the fish, thinking they would make a welcome change to the muddy taste of catfish from the paddy fields.

Ahead in the distance he recognised the silhouette of Pak Wan's boy sitting in his usual place beneath the mango tree, his knees pulled up towards his chin, his skinny arms wrapped around his legs, staring out over the luminous green fields of rice. Sometimes the boy would rock back and forth and make low moaning sounds, but today he was silent and unmoving.

Almost every family in the village had a child that was an outcast, or who was hidden like a shameful burden, kept in a back room, or sometimes outside in a pen, like an animal, living, eating and sleeping in its own waste. Some said it was part of the curse upon the island, but he knew that it was much simpler than that.

Last week he found the boy crouched on his hands and knees beside the calf in the lean-to behind his house, sucking on one of the buffalo's spare teats. It surprised him that the boy managed to compete with the greedy calf, who always wanted more, butting its mother's udder with its head.

A few months earlier he had walked halfway across the island with the buffalo to have her sired. It took him two whole days, one there and one back, and cost him a month's worth of rice, but it was either that or risk another stillbirth. It was an investment in the future.

He watched the suckling boy for a moment, then quietly stepped away. Let the boy drink what he could. There was hunger in the village. Those who contributed the least were the last to be fed. The boy contributed nothing. Nothing except heartache.

It was almost a year since the boy ambushed a girl on her way back from the fields. She lost the baby, whether naturally, or by an infusion of herbs gathered in the forest, no one knew. It wasn't the sort of thing that was talked about.

The girl's father came to see him. He talked about the rice harvest, and then about the lack of rain, working up his courage towards what he really wanted to say. You have a daughter of your own, surely you must understand. He nodded. He understood.

Some of the villagers wanted to kill the boy, he was a risk to their daughters too, but he spoke against it.

The boy wasn't right to begin with, he argued. He had less sense than a billy-goat. Besides, if they had to kill all those in the village who weren't right ...

He left the sentence unfinished, but still he was there that night they stuffed the rag into the boy's frightened mouth. When the girl's father lowered the heated knife he wanted to put his hands over his ears to block out the stifled screams, but instead he gritted his teeth and pushed the boy's shoulders down into the ground.

"I got some fish and lots of eggs."

His wife looked up. She and their daughter were in the small plot behind the sun-bleached wooden house, bent over the bed of new rice seedling green. She stood up, placed her hands on her hips and arched back groaning, rubbing her lower back and pounding it with the sides of her fists.

He stood watching his daughter, the way her hips shifted as she worked. Though she kept its innocence, she had lost the awkward jerkiness of childhood. Now there was a smooth assuredness in her movements and a confident stillness in her eyes. He was proud of her. She was smart and obedient and she was a good worker. He wanted to say something about the sown seeds being the seeds of the future, but he couldn't work out the right words in his head. Instead he said nothing.

His wife watched him watching the girl. He turned his gaze towards her and then towards his feet.

"A shipful of sailors landed today," he said. "Their boat needs some repairs. They'll be on the island for a few days."

Husband and wife stood shoulder to shoulder looking out towards the hills on the horizon while upper teeth worried lower lips.

"Need to get the far field ploughed if we're to get these seedlings in," she said.

"I was planning on doing it now."

He untethered the buffalo and rope-led her towards the fields. She looked back with a whining grunt, reassuring her calf that she would return he guessed. The calf was getting stronger every day. By next year it would be bigger than its mother and would take over the role of pulling the plough.

He bundled his sarong up around his waist, revealing his thin sinewy legs. He stepped into the sun-heated water of the paddy field. The warm mud beneath it oozed up between his toes and around his ankles. The ploughshare slid through the fermenting viscous muck, releasing bubbles of gas that smelled of childhood memories of when his father ploughed this field as well. He had made the ploughshare himself, from a piece of hardwood from the forest. Shaping it had blunted his parang several times. He worked back and forth across the field with the buffalo until the sun was low. He was tired, but the field was ready. Tomorrow the planting could begin.

THE DAUGHTER WALKED in front of her parents. She was the only one left now. Their future depended entirely on her. They had lost three other children. All daughters. Two never made it beyond the first month of confinement, but it took nearly three years to understand that there was something wrong with the third, something wrong that could never be made right. She died in her sleep. She hardly even struggled.

The family worked side by side, sweating in the humid heat, pressing the slender seedlings into the warm nourishing mud. With luck and rain, their work would ensure their survival for another season.

They finished before the hottest part of the day. They washed and ate and rested in the shade.

HIS WIFE STAYED BEHIND at the home. Standing in the protective shade of the mango tree she watched them leave, her fingers knotting and unknotting, following them with her eyes along the trail that led towards the river until they were out of sight.

He saw that there were other fathers with their daughters at the river too, and some men with their wives. He recognised them all, but none would meet his eye, ignoring him, but without hostility, their eyes turned inwards, absorbed in their own thoughts. After some brief haggling over the price, they all boarded the wooden sampan that would carry them downstream to the sea.

He watched the boatman position himself, standing on a raised platform at the back of the little wooden boat. He pushed the bamboo pole against the riverbed, but the seaward current did most of the hard work. It was the return journey that would be harder. For everyone. The surface of the river rippled as the boat glided forward, and each time the tip of the pole splashed free of the water he saw sunlight transform the shining droplets into molten silvery jewels.

Unlike their fathers, the girls did not behave as strangers to one another. As children they had played together, but now that they were budding women they rarely had the chance to meet. They were kept busy with cooking and laundry and hard work in the gardens and the fields. Most of them were cousins. Their youthful features looked so alike that a stranger might mistake them all for sisters. They were excited. Even though the walk from the village to the ocean was only half a day they seldom had occasion to visit the island's coast. Their carefree laughter and chatter filled the late afternoon, echoing across the water and through the trees as the boat smoothly slipped downstream.

The girls walked out onto the fine white sand, mesmerised by the sunlight twinkling on the vast ocean. The waves made a hushing sound, like whispered secrets that they could not understand.

At the edge of the forest, the sailors had slung hammocks in the shade. Smells of wood smoke and cooking drifted from a fire set upon the sand. Some of the men played music, twanging on homemade stringed instruments, beating goatskin drums, or whistling on little flutes. Others were busy cutting meat, a rare delicacy for men so used to eating fish.

He counted almost twenty of them. They were a mixed bunch. No two looked alike. Even without hearing their strange accents, any islander would know that they were outsiders.

He spotted the man who had given him the fish and nodded. The sailor stepped out from behind the veil of smoke that rose above the cooking fire.

He called his daughter. She came and stood by his side.

He felt hatred towards this brute of a man, the man who had given him four shining fish. He couldn't face seeing his daughter eat them in the end, so he had given them to Pak Wan's hungry boy instead.

He lightly placed his hand in the curve of his daughter's lower back, realising with a sudden sharp intensity that he had never loved the girl as intensely as he did right now. He asked himself how it was possible to feel so much anger and so much love at the same time. He held his hand on the girl's back for a moment longer, then with the gentlest touch he nudged her forward.

The sailor roughly took her hand. The look of confusion on her face changed to horrified understanding. She resisted at first, but her father nodded, while he clenched teeth and fists. His daughter's expression would be branded on his mind forever. He tasted the sour saltiness of blood inside his mouth. He had bitten through his lip. It occurred to him that he was standing almost on the exact spot where he had gathered Penyu's eggs. He swallowed the metallic taste, and watched the stranger lead his daughter away towards the trees.

Five-Star Experience

It was still dark when Nuraliza left the house. She was working the morning shift all week, so Ajis would have to dress and take the children to school. She knew he didn't mind. He was a good father. She tucked the ends of her tudung into the neck of her long-sleeved tee-shirt so that it wouldn't flap around in the wind. The helmet pulled the cloth in tight against her ears, muffling the sound of the waves as she drove along the coast.

She nodded to the other women as they parked their motosikals near the staff entrance of the hotel. Some of them were already wearing their uniforms, but Nuraliza preferred to change in the locker room. It drew a line between her job and her life outside the hotel.

The fluorescent light in the housekeeping office flashed and hummed a few times before settling down. She picked up an empty rattan basket from the shelf and went out into the grey light of the garden, swatting mosquitoes away while she gathered fallen frangipani blossoms and plucked fragrant jasmine from the bushes. It wasn't a bad way to start the day, but sometimes she disturbed lizards and was always wary of interrupting the slumber of a sleeping snake. Later the flowers would be delicately placed on the crisp white cotton pillows of each guest's freshly-made bed.

Back in the office she transferred the flowers into a plastic tub, sealed it and then put it in the refrigerator so that they would remain fresh. She took another larger plastic box down from a shelf. Its contents rattled inside.

The carved granite paving stones wound past the fountains and lotus ponds, then around the edge of the infinity pool and down the steps onto the beach. She kicked off her shoes and let the fine sand cool her feet. In just a few hours' time this same sand would be too hot to walk on. Most of it had been brought here on a barge, mined from the pristine beaches of some of the other uninhabited islands within the archipelago.

The sea whispered greetings as Nuraliza walked along the shore. She took seashells from the box and dropped them on the sand. Some were local shells, cones and conches, whelks and seriths, others like the nautilus, or the seahorses and the starfish were bought wholesale, imported from the Philippines.

Sarah and David Vanderbilt-Roth got chatting with the Blyton-Smythes over cocktails at the poolside bar and continued their conversation over dinner.

"This is our second honeymoon," said Sarah. "The last one was over twenty years ago, sailing along the coast of Maine."

"Sarah's the romantic," said David. "I just call it a vacation. What about you folks?"

"Our granddaughter came here on her gap year," said Janice Blyton-Smythe. "It was her photos that convinced us to give this part of the world a chance. She was travelling around with a back-pack, if you can believe that. She's always been an adventurous young soul. That's all well and good when one is young, but we really wanted something a little more... how should I put it? Safe?"

"Safe. Yes, well, I'm just glad to be on dry land again," said David. "I've decided I'm too old to be a sailor."

"Been sailing then, David, have we?" asked Janice's husband Dennis. "Never really was much tempted by that. Life on the ocean wave, what?"

"Yes, we've just spent a week island-hopping around the Andaman Sea," said Sarah, answering for her husband. "We sailed down all the way from Phuket. Not quite sure if that's how you say it. David insists on pronouncing the pee-haitch like an eff."

"It's not just the name of the place," said David leaning forward. "It's a whole attitude. From what I've seen it encapsulates the whole stress-free ethos of the tropics. 'Fuck it'. What could be simpler than that?"

"Oh darling, please behave."

"I am behaving."

"Yes, but badly."

"Ah, fuck it. Let's order another bottle of wine."

"I'll second that," said Dennis with a laugh.

"What about the poverty?" asked Janice. "Did you see much of that?"

"Oh, we didn't go ashore much. At least nowhere inhabited. We passed a few fishermen in their boats. They were smiling. I suppose they are happy."

"Yes, the locals really do seem remarkably resilient," said Janice. "It just goes to show that money can't buy happiness."

"No, it can't," said David. "But if I'm going to be miserable, I'd rather be miserable in luxury."

Dessert was followed by coffee. David and Dennis ordered brandy.

"I'm going to call it a night," said Sarah. "Don't stay up too late darling. You know you'll regret it in the morning."

Janice smiled unsteadily and left the table too, tottering precariously on her heels.

"Aw, fuck it!" said David after the women had left. "Let's have another round."

SARAH WOKE up early and couldn't get back to sleep. David lay beside her, snoring. She would let him sleep it off. She stepped into the shower and used the complimentary Caswell-Massey soap. This really was the five-star experience. After, she put on a light cotton dress and went out for a walk.

The sun was just coming up, painting the ocean shades of pink and peach. She walked along the sand, a gentle breeze tugging at her hair. She had the whole beach to herself. Evidently, the hotel's guests were not early risers, though there had been an old but energetic man in black swimming shorts thrashing up and down the pool. She stooped to pick up a shell. It was beautifully patterned. Then she saw another one. Soon she had more shells than she could hold in her hands, each one more enticing than the last. She held up the hem of her dress and put the shells in the little hollow of the cloth.

She came back to the room with more than a dozen shells. David was still snoring but had moved over to her side of the bed, just like he always did at home. She went into the bathroom and arranged the shells in a line on the marble countertop. That looked too orderly and neat. She broke up the line and tried to find a more artistic arrangement.

She was still busy with the shells when David came into the bathroom. His eyes were bloodshot, but he managed a weak smile.

"Been shopping?"

"No, these were gifts from the ocean. Aren't they beautiful?"

David picked up one of the larger ones and held it to his ear.

"I think it's a wrong number, but it might be for you," he said handing her the shell.

"You're still drunk, aren't you?"

"I haven't quite decided yet. Let me take a shower and then I'll tell you. What are you going to do with all these shells anyway?"

"I suppose I'll have to leave them here. I think customs would confiscate them if I tried to bring them home."

"Yeah, whatever," he sighed with a wave of his hand.

"Would you prefer room service for breakfast? We could get them to serve it on the patio. Or we could eat in one of the restaurants."

"I think I'll pass on breakfast. Maybe just a glass of juice. There might be some in the minibar."

"Well, I hope we can have breakfast together tomorrow. It will be our last day. I really want to make the most of this five-star experience."

"Your whole life is a five-star experience, honey. Anyway, let me take that shower."

The following afternoon the Vanderbilt-Roths checked out of the hotel. A driver took them to the airport in an air-conditioned limousine and helped them check in for their long-haul first-class flights.

Nuraliza had nearly finished her shift. There was just one last room left to clean. It had been a late check-out. She found the shells on the countertop in the bathroom, arranged in a spiral, placed in order of size with the smallest at the centre. She gathered them up in a used hand towel.

Back in the housekeeping office she transferred the shells into the plastic box. Tomorrow she would put them back on the beach for other new five-star guests to find.

Bamboo Swing

The wavering light of kerosene lamps dotted through the darkness of the valley mirrored the twinkling stars above. She waited for him by the dark silhouette of the bamboo swing. They sat, the loop of rope forcing them close together, their feet scraping the ground as they swayed.

As children they had swung here, screaming at the dizzying excitement of the centrifugal force as their feet faced the sky. Now other forces worked upon and within them. The darkness hid their blushing faces, his acne-ridden skin and their fumbling first kiss - a trembling brushing of lips, an awkward clashing of teeth, the unsteady rocking of their bodies on the swing.

Prashant's walkie-talkie crackled. A suspected shoplifting in the women's underwear section. Again. There must be about the temptation of women's underwear that turned people into thieves.

The suspect was a corpulent middle-aged woman. She wore a headscarf, a tight white t-shirt and black elastic leggings that did everything to highlight but little to flatter her natural curves.

Prashant stepped in front of her, blocking her way in the toothpaste aisle. Mouthwash. Dental Floss. Toothbrushes.

"Please, bag opening," he said.

This was usually when they started shouting in indignation, often with racial slurs thrown in for good measure, questioning his right to come to their country and make such ludicrous accusations. But instead, the woman just meekly opened her handbag and slowly removed its contents one by one. She handed Prashant the empty bag as if daring him to find anything.

He returned the bag with a nod that was part apology, part admission that the woman had somehow duped the system. Perhaps she had an accomplice, or had gotten cold feet and dumped whatever camera three had seen her take.

Though unfruitful and anti-climactic the false alarm was the highlight of Prashant's entire week. For a few tiny moments he had almost felt a sense of purpose. Then everything returned to the usual monotonous tedium of counting the hours remaining until it was time to clock out and he could rest his aching feet.

He stood at the entry to the shop, watching the shoppers, some shopping for windows, some shopping for real – families, couples, but especially young women. His eyes couldn't resist following their movements, like the security cameras recording the details of their clothing, their hair, their skin, all to be longingly replayed in private later in the hostel he called home.

Those recordings always inevitably brought him back to the same place - to the village, to smooth-skinned Anjali and the cold autumn evening on the bamboo swing.

All over the hillsides and valleys bamboo was cut in preparation for the autumn festival of Daishan. Four poles were lashed together at the top, forming a four-legged tripod, a quadropod, the feet firmly anchored in the claggy post-monsoon clay. The looped rope hung down ready to receive anyone who dared defy gravity. The children had to be supervised at first so that everyone got their turn, but after a day or two the initial novelty wore off and anyone could use the swing.

The smell of fresh bamboo and the tautness of the rope across his buttocks came back to Prashant as clearly as Anjali beside him. And yet try as he might he couldn't conjure up her face, only details – the hair half-covering her cheekbone, the plumpness of her lower lip, the sparkle of her eyes.

He let out a shuddering sigh. One year, two months and twelve days left and he would be free again. Then his employer would return his passport and he could return to the mountains of Nepal.

Without his passport he had no freedom. It felt like a prison term, serving out the sentence of self-imposed exile. He felt caged, trapped, and the only way out was back to the place he had tried to escape.

He had mixed feelings about going home to Nepal again. He had done so once before, thinking he would return with a pocket full of money and a suitcase full of presents and settle down and marry Anjali. During three years of tropical heat he had dreamt of returning to the fresh mountain air and falling into her awaiting arms. Instead he discovered that she was pregnant and married to a boy from the next village. When she saw Prashant she turned her head away.

Having barely unpacked his bags he repacked them again, along with his memories of the evening on the swing, using part of his hard-earned cash to return to Malaysia.

It would be autumn in Nepal by now, the leaves changing colour, the crops on the terraced slopes ready for harvest. He could almost smell the sweet rot of decomposing leaves, feel the cold chill of the air.

He moved out of the reach of the cold air blasting down from the air-conditioning unit at the entrance of the shop. Here it was still summer. Here it was always summer, a permanent unchanging season with nothing to mark one day from the next. Days repeated themselves with the irritating regularity of an over-played CD stuck, caught, repeating the same few notes, discordant and disconnected to the original melody, a melody interrupted by the bitter-sweetness of Anjali's whispered broken promises, leaving him with fading echoes of something lost forever in a time and place that could no longer exist, an unassuageable yearning – like the unscratchable itch of a phantom limb. Yet despite the hurt the echoes warmed him with the reassurance of who he had once been, and he realised at last that it wasn't Anjali or the mountains that he missed, but himself.

Ah Girl Wants a Vaccine

Frenz Group

Wendy, Julie, Angie, Linda, Kimmy ...

135 Unread Messages

Denise Leong

You all want to get vaccine ahnot? Takut.

Wendy Loke

You takut vaccine but not takut cronavirus? Liddat osso kan ah?

Julie Kee

Big Pharma lah. Money making scam.

Kimmy Wong

Lab virus

Grace Chong

What is Lab virus? I tot Corona, like the beer?

Kimmy Wong

Designer virus

Julie Kee

China virus

Wendy Loke

Kepala otak. Bukan China virus. Bat punya virus.

Ah Girl

I want, but how to make appointment?

Amy Ong

You must guna MySayasalah app

Ah Girl

I know. I download already but I don't understand it.

Amy Ong

First you open the app

Ah Girl

Okay

Amy Ong

Then you see the tiny button where it says 'close'?

Ah Girl

Yes, so tiny. Big button more expensive or what?

Amy Ong

You need to press that

Ah Girl

But I want to open the app, not close it

Amy Ong

I know. It doesn't make sense but to open it you need to press 'close' and then you get a whole lot of different options.

Ah Girl

Close means open?

Amy Ong

Yeah

Eva Teng

Rilly?

Amy Ong

Yeah

Ah Girl

Close, but not close enough

Eva Teng

Who design this piece of shit? They never hear of UI.

Grace Chong

UI. My doctor want to give me one of them. She say for sure I won't get pregnant and it's less harmful than the pill.

Amy Ong

That's an IUD you're thinking of

Grace Chong

Oh, sorry right. UI, IUD. Same same.

Linda Tay

UI? More like UTI

Joanne Chee

Is that a university?

Linda Tay

No lah, urinary tract infection.

Joanne Chee

What's that to do with the MySayasalah app?

Eva Teng

Aiyah u gaiz. UI is User Interface

Ah Girl

Useless Interface more like it

Wendy Loke

Seven million dollar they pay for that you know

Joanne Chee

It's a nice colour blue

Ah Girl

So is the sky, but you get that one for free

Eva Teng

Nehmind the app lah. Got one online competition for AB vaccine soon.

Joanne Chee

Must wait until the old people are vaccinated first. Flatliners too.

Eva Teng

Flatliners?

Joanne Chee

Frontliners. Autocorrect. Shirt. Fuschia. Hate this phone.

Jessie Chin

AB competition how to enter? Got entry fee or not?

Eva Teng

No fee. It's not a competition, it's a lottery

Wendy Loke

Lottery, competition, same difference

Joanne Chee

Lottery is gambling. Haram, no? That mean we have a better chance to win?

Julie Kee

Gahmen want to give you something for free you want to take it? Sheeple just do what your told? You really trust these buggers?

Kimmy Wong

AB Yahudi agenda.

Ah Girl

Rubbish. Who told you that?

Kimmy Wong

My aunt share from her Wazzarp group.

Eva Teng

AB from Oxford lah. England where got yahudi agenda one? Yehudi Menuhin more like

Joanne Chee

Is that another vaccine? Got so many name cannot keep track

Eva Teng

He's a violinist lah. You never listen to music?

Ah Girl

Like what's her name?

Eva Teng

Who?

Ah Girl

You know, the Singapore girl

Joanne Chee

An air hostess?

Ah Girl

Aiyah. Not that kind of Singapore girl. The violin one.

Eva Teng

Vanessa Mae

Jessie Chin

Who's she?

Eva Teng

The Singaporean violinist? You donno?

Wendy Loke

U gaiz all talk cock only. How to enter the AB lottery? If can have a chance to win I for sure want to buy a number.

Eva Teng

You need to use this link

Grace Chong

What link?

Joanne Chee

There's a link?

Ah Girl

More like a missing link

Jessie Chin

Hello, Eva. Got link or not?

Eva Teng

Sorry, I osso chatting in one other group.

Joanne Chee

What group?

Eva Teng

Nehmind.

Ah Girl

Hello? Vaccine lottery link?

Eva Teng

Here.

www.kerajaan/gov/user/kat/mana/ABvaccine/register/en/

Joanne Chee

For sure this the official one? Looks fishy to me

Julie Kee

It is fishy. Why you think they want to give it away. No one want this yahudi vaccine

Eva Teng

Don't start with that yahudi thing again. Oxford, okay. Oxford in England, like Inspector Morse

Joanne Chee

Who?

Ah Girl

He's a friend with Vanessa Mae

Grace Chong

Rilly?

Ah Girl

No lah. Joking

Grace Chong

Not funny.

Ah Girl

I'm laughing

Grace Chong

I'm not

Ah Girl

I prefer the young Morse. Endeavour. Cuter.

Wendy Loke

Why you don't watch Korean drama like a normal person?

Ah Girl

Because I understand English and I don't understand Korean

Kimmy Wong

But they are more like us

Eva Teng

Where got?

Grace Chong

I click the link and it opens a page and say must only play on Sunday at 2pm sharp.

Angie Low

But if you don play how? I got church meeting Sunday 2pm.

Eva Teng

Cancel lah

Joanne Chee

Pandemic you still go to church?

Angie Low

WFH lah

Grace Chong

What is WFH?

Linda Tay

Wife For Hire

Grace Chong

For hire to do what?

Linda Tay

What you think? Hanky Panky.

Eva Teng

Angie, your church got hanky panky issit?

Wendy Loke

Every church got hanky panky. U donno?

Angie Low

No lah. Just a meeting of the committee to organize distribution of essential items to the needy

Grace Chong

What essential items?

Angie Low

Food, pampers, cooking oil, eggs, all that. You want to help you all are welcome.

Grace Chong

I will help. I PM you.

Joanne Chee

PM? You mean DM?

Linda Tay

PM is premenstrual. You know why she write that.

Joanne Chee

I thought it was Prime Minister

Amy Ong

Joanne, sanction. Against group rules. You know we don't talk about that kind of thing. You never know who could be reading.

Ah Girl

PM is perimenopause

Wendy Loke

Hamaigad, so much to look forward to

Joanne Chee

Who else is playing lottery on Sunday

Jessie Chin

Got lottery? I thought everything closed down

Joanne Chee

Scroll up. Gahmen got haram lottery for vaccines prizes, but AB only.

Jessie Chin

AB? No Flyzer?

Eva Teng

Notchet.

Jessie Chin

I want Flyzer.

Linda Tay

Got too may side effects. Sinoharm much better

Grace Chong

Sinoharm the same as Sinohack?

Joanne Chee

Sinohack the 5G one

Wendy Loke

My phone got 4G only

Joanne Chee

Then you cannot get Sinohack

Linda Tay

It's the other way around. Sinohack gives you 5G

Grace Chong

What is 5G anyway?

Joanne Chee

5G good 4D better

Linda Tay

Good Girls Get Gropy Ghosts

Amy Ong

Gropy?

Linda Tay

Okay, Groaning

Amy Ong

Groaning Ghosts? Why?

Linda Tay

Hanky Panky

Amy Ong

With ghosts?

Linda Tay

I'd try

Eva Teng

We know you would

Jessie Chin

Anyone know how to work this MySayasalah app? My son download for me

Ah Girl

Just press 'close'

Jessie Chin

But I want to open it

Ah Girl

To open you need to press 'close'

Jessie Chin

Srsly? That makes like zero sense.

Eva Teng

Come on ugaiz. Not this shit again

Dr. Fintan

Net-bagged bottles of Mekong-cooled Chang trailed in the murky water, ballast to the rudderless rubber tubes cushioning us wet-arsed downstream. The riverbanks slid lazily past, tangled undergrowth bannered with tattered strips of flood-swept plastic, a posse of barefooted children diligently playing or fishing by the water's edge, bamboo canes for rods. Others squatted in the shade of tin-roofed shacks, picking nits from each other's hair. They jumped up when they caught sight of us, calling and laughing and waving, flashing white teeth. I tried to imagine kids on the banks of the Liffey or Dodder. They'd probably throw rocks. I took a last slug of lukewarm beer and tossed the empty bottle in close to the bank. A flurry of limbs splashed to retrieve it. Bottles better than cans, Mr Phang had said. The children would take them to be recycled and earn a few coins, which might have explained why they seemed happy to see us. I watched the fastest boy, wet black hair matted, skin shining, grinning as he held the dripping green bottle aloft. I waved good-bye, feeling an uncomfortable mix of munificence and shame, and let the current sweep the children out of sight, but not out of mind.

"Here," croaked Dr Fintan, our tubes bumping together in a

buoyant kiss, yielding for a moment before rebounding in slow motion. I reached for the joint, and with arms extended we momentarily became Michelangelo's Creation of Adam. I took a few long hits, head tilted back, and watched the slow ominous expansion of giant cumulus cauliflowers. Gnarled banyans streamed aerial roots down from their dark leafy crowns, then the riverbanks became green barcodes and barcodes and barcodes of bamboo.

Maria. I tried to conjure up her voice, the faint Spanish lisp, the elision of her vowels over the years, from Dough-bleen to Duh-blun. I lib in a billage, she once said when we first met. Mah-Ree-a, she insisted, not Mar-eeya. Gin and tonic accents, her voice just out of reach. Maria saying I don't want another thirty forty fifty years of this. Maria saying I don't want to pretend anymore. I felt her words, more than heard them. I tried to reconstruct her face, superimpose it against the clouds, against the inside of my eyelids, but all I got were fragments: the tapered nape of her neck, the rounded curve of a cheekbone, the dotted stubble between and around her eyebrows, the plucked hair growing back. Or was it new hair? The word follicles flickered past. I tried to grasp it, tried to see her face, but it was like water trickling between my fingers. The only half-clear image I could conjure up was her Facebook profile photo, unchanged for years. She never used her account. No recent activity either, I had checked. And checked. Maria, frozen in the moment, surreptitiously saved to my phone, arm draped around her childhood friend Carmen's shoulder, both raising beer glasses, eyes double-glazed, faces toilet-flushed, skin shining in the unforgiving light of camera flash. There are blurred figures in the dark background, splashes of purple and yellow light. I tried to remember where the photo was taken. Had I been there? Did I take the photo? I thought maybe I did, but couldn't be sure that it wasn't a false memory. Perhaps the seven-year-long episode of our lives together was a false memory too – seven years phantom itching to be scratched. I had nothing to show for it, everything left behind, all stolen by time, that most skilled of thieves who loots our lives and fences the damaged goods piecemeal to memory, phantom fragments meted out in ghostly glimpses.

I opened my eyes. The early evening light had turned sulphuric yellow. I levered myself as upright as possible, the black rubber complaining. My back ached. I trailed my hand in the warm water, splashed some on my face. Mr Phang was just ahead, pointing to a rickety wooden jetty nestled in a shadowed bend of the river.

A man on the jetty held a looped blue nylon rope that uncoiled as it sailed through the air. Mr Phang caught it, using the current to hold it taut. He gestured with his free hand, urging us to grab hold of the rope. Our tubes bumped against each other, and one by one we were helped ashore by wiry shirtless teenagers, waist-deep in the brown muddy water. Solid ground. More or less. I stumbled, my inner ear still floating on the river, my coordination impaired by the beers.

One of the Swedes, Sven, or Jens – I couldn't get their names straight – failed to understand and drifted past, spinning in an eddy, looking comically lost as the current pulled him away. He and his friend were in competition to see which could sustain more chemical impairment and still stay conscious. A wiry youth launched himself in pursuit. Despite his bent-limbed splashes he was an efficient swimmer. The Swede flung himself on the boy, embracing a human being whose whole existence he had been unaware of mere moments before in an instinctive act of trust. Or maybe he merely saw the boy as a human lifeboat. The boy shouted something the Swede failed to understand. They struggled with the intimacy of lovers until the boy finally managed to stand up and the Swede finally understood that the muddy water in which he so feared drowning was barely waist deep. We all cheered as they both staggered muddily to the shore.

My travelling companions' faces glowed in varying shades of sunburn and drunkenness. Someone cracked open the last few bottles of Chang. Another in a day-long line of joints was passed around. We fell silent, contemplative, engaging in a reverential ritual older than history, slapping whining mosquitoes, as a huge satsuma orange sun quickly slid behind the black silhouettes of the coconut palms on the opposite bank.

Mr Phang was our double-dee, our designated driver, the one who stayed sober and made sure we safely reached our destination. All the way down river he had kept a waterproof bag slung across his chest, guarding our passports and wallets. He wanted to keep our phones dry as well, but no one wanted to pass up on taking the photos we planned to upload the moment we found a decent WiFi signal. In the half-light we watched him finish the joint and flick the fizzing roach into the river. He distributed wallets, flipped open our passports and passed them to us one by one. I slipped mine into my shirt pocket. Dr Fintan, more precautious, lifted his shirt and zipped his inside a money belt.

It was a short walk uphill to the hostel. As we walked Dr Fintan gave an impromptu lecture on river-borne diseases: cholera, typhoid, dysentery, hep A. I hadn't taken any shots, but unlike the Swedes I had no fresh tattoos to infect, and for once no knife-nicks or oil-spatter blisters. We listened to Dr Fintan expound, with the devotion of disciples. He was a charismatic charmer who apparently maintained his reassuring bedside manner no matter how much he drank. There are people you meet in life who bring you up, who seem eager to believe the best about you, and others who bring you down. Fintan was resolutely in the former category and when he listened it was as if you were imparting hard-won wisdom or some nugget of information that utterly fascinated him. But he could turn this on with anyone, and then you felt less special, manipulated somehow, betrayed and disappointed, but ironically more disappointed in yourself than him.

Our backpacks had made it to the hostel as promised. We paid Mr Phang his cash-on-delivery and slapped him on the back, promising to fill the internet with rave reviews, then watched him climb into the cab of the pick-up truck that would take him and the tied and tamed stack of tubes back up river, ready for the same trip again the following day with another group of green inebriated travellers.

We bagged bunks in a dank dormitory that already reeked of sunblock, pot, and musky male sweat. I had met Fintan a few days earlier in a dormitory just like this. "You Irish?" he asked in a lilting Cork accent, pointing towards the tricolour clumsily stitched to my backpack. "Just heading out for beers and grub with a few of the lads like. Join us?" We had been travelling together since, part of a raggle-taggle group of unshaven young men struggling to grow proper hipster beards, with varying degrees of failure or success.

Events might have transpired differently if I hadn't lain down after my shower, but we can rarely identify the precise points where our lives veer course until after the fact. I heard Fintan's voice filtered through the grimy mosquito net. "Pizza?" he asked, voice rising sharply on the second syllable. Eyes closed, head reeling from my excessive absorption of beer and grass and reflected river light, I mumbled a vague reply about catching up later.

I woke under the harsh neon to the trance rhythm of the ceiling fan. I was groggy and dry-mouthed, still half-drunk half-stoned, eyes gritty sun-dried raisins, a vicious pounding pain pile-driving through my head. I popped a few painkillers, thirstily emptied my water bottle and took another shower to cool off and wash away a newly accumulated layer of sticky sweat. The dormitory was empty. Outside, frogs and insects sang. Motorcycles and tuk-tuks buzzed past, dopplering into the distance. I reached into my backpack, already sweating again despite my shower, and extracted my notebook and pen. I sat on the bed flicking through the first few scrawled pages. The record of my trip stalled abruptly somewhere mid-air after Abu Dhabi with a rhetorical inquiry as to why airline food always contained red and green bell peppers. I uncapped my pen. I recalled the silent square-faced immigration clerk, but couldn't remember the name of the airport. I flicked through my passport looking for the entry stamp. A moment of confusion, then a realisation: This was Fintan's passport. Mr Phang must have switched them by mistake. It was easy to see how it had happened. We had already been mistaken for brothers several times, one matronly hostel owner shrugging, saying, "All you Irish look same same."

I could have gone out to look for him, or just kept writing in my notebook and waited for his return. Instead I slipped the passport back into my pocket, shut my notebook, capped my pen, climbed out from beneath the mosquito net, found my sandals, looped my backpack straps over my shoulders, and walked out the side door of the dormitory into the humid frog-chirping night.

I hadn't walked far when I heard a tuk-tuk approach. I stopped in a puddle of flickering yellow light beneath a streetlamp and flagged it down. Twenty minutes later I was gazing into the darkness beyond my reflection in the window of a night train headed to the coast.

The repetitive clack-clacking of the rails and the gentle swaying of the train must have rocked me off to sleep. It was still dark when I awoke, the landscape outside still invisible. My neck was stiff. I had drooled down my chin. I wiped my face with the back of my hand and looked around in confusion, not yet fully understanding or remembering where I was. The carriage was three quarters empty, all the other passengers asleep. I noted with relief that no one had stolen my backpack while I slept. The muzziness of my hangover acted as a buffer, cushioning the facts, allowing an uneasy acceptance of what I had done to sink in. It wasn't too late to turn around. I could get off at the next station, make the return trip. But I knew I wouldn't. The voice that urged me to backpedal belonged to someone else, someone I used to be.

The sky brightened on the horizon, followed by a ballooning sun that rose into the cloudless sky as quickly as it had set. I half-opened a window, inviting a cool morning breeze to sweep through the carriage and sooth my sun-burned face. Despite a precautionary slathering of factor-fifty before the river trip I was starting to peel. My fingers explored the tender flaking skin, relishing the delicate peeling off of sun-cooked epidermal layers, fingers gradually growing more insistent, I was helpless to resist, tearing through the chrysalis, pulling away the mask. Like a snake I was shedding skin, sloughing off a former self, becoming Dr Fintan.

THE WAVES WERE unenthusiastic lapping things, the ocean as lethargic as the waiters sitting in the back, heads resting on folded forearms. Earlier I had crossed the coal-hot sand to test the water. It was bathtub warm. The midday sun was too scorching for my raw and ravaged face, so I sat sweating on a plastic chair in the airless, breezeless shade, a glass of beer before me on a plastic table, feet half-hidden in soft warm sand, listening to a Bob Dylan compilation piped through cheap speakers that looked and sounded as though they had been salvaged from a car-wreck. I watched a fly describe aerial arabesques and come to rest on the rim of my beer glass. I waved my hand, it disappeared, reappeared, I waved my hand again. This went on for ... how long? A few minutes? Half an hour? All afternoon?

I counted the seconds before it landed again – 12, 27, 3, 19, 5 - counting heartbeats measured out in fly-time, the ticking of my heart-clock winding down towards an inevitable stop, counting the precious seconds left, the precious seconds left, the precious seconds left: uncertain and unknowable in number, but countable all the same. How many? millions? a billion? more? less? I made mental calculations searching for patterns in the numbers, divining the intervals between them, looking for answers, wondering at the forgotten definitions of words like integers and prime numbers. But fly numerology was no more useful or informative than random strings of letters forming nonsense words.

I emptied my glass, understanding even less than at my first edge-cutting sip, concluding that flies, like much in life, obey obscure principles; we are all subjects to the whims and inscrutable reign and rule of randomness. Time was running out - for the fly, for me - one life lived already, time to make the most of the new life I had stolen. But first I had to find out who I was.

Despite my scepticism a Google search revealed that I really was a doctor, a proper medical doctor, on sabbatical from a Waterford hospital, volunteering my time with MSF, certainly a step up the slippery ring-rang-rungs of the social laddered stocking from a lowly cook fanning flames and delicate culinary egos in a fashionably over-priced Dublin restaurant. I tried to recall anything I knew about medicine. Treating burns and dressing wounds – tick. Been there, done that. I had once packaged and preserved a colleague's severed finger in a Tupperware of ice, hardly an incredible exploit, but the finger was eventually successfully reattached, albeit with a certain loss of sensation. My only time in hospital, that I could remember, was to have my stomach pumped after a particularly wild night out, though my much-maligned mother assured me that I was born in a hospital in the Coombe, the word umbilically tied and rhymed to womb. From womb to Coombe, the difference of a hard or soft consonant. Right-click, define - a narrow valley or deep hollow, especially one enclosed on all but one side. Indeed. Birth in the Liberties a narrow liberation. Apart from that I had little experience of the medical world, though I must surely have absorbed something through osmosis and exposure to Maria's binge-watching of ER and Doctor House, perhaps even a sub-conscious desire to pander to her viewing habits.

I checked Dr Fintan's Facebook page. His last post was a selfie taken on the river, captioned: turn off your mind, relax, and float downstream ...#gowiththeflow #imlivinit. No mention of a stolen passport. Maybe he was oblivious and still carried mine snugly tucked against his belly. I went as far as clicking on the message option, my finger hovering for a moment. Dear Fintan, I wrote, hesitating when I saw the words on the screen, not knowing whether I had made a Freudian slip. Only two vowels difference between Dr and Dear. A before E except after D. A&E: Accident and Emergency. A sign? I deleted the clumsy debut, closed the tab, and started looking for my next destination. I needed somewhere to lie low. If I played my cards right my newly acquired volunteer visa was good for a full year of tropical heat, time enough to weigh my options.

I was momentarily distracted by a group of four Swedish girls – women — young women, settling themselves down around a table. They looked pretty in a group, less so when examined individually. Always the way, but why? What tricks do our brains play, and why? Here, is there anyone at all between the ages of eighteen and twenty-five left in Sweden? I wanted to say. Yiz all seem to be in South East Asia. But I kept all my questions to myself, greedily hoarding them, perhaps for future use. Not that I meant to be ungenerous, but the less I had to do with women the better. The thought inevitably led me back to Maria. The whole point of my trip had been to leave her behind, yet I carried her with me everywhere. She was minding my books while I was away; boxes and boxes of them, the only thing I wanted to salvage. She could keep the rest, including the Ikea furniture - especially the Ikea furniture. I mourned precious hours of life lost wandering that Swedish labyrinth. Join the Billy-club to beat yourself with. Sweden again. Maybe it was the girls, women, whatever, triggering flat-pack memories. What tricks do our brains play, and why?

A wild-haired local, with mirror sunglasses and a ragged red t-shirt that said Santana in faded letters, strolled through the restaurant as if gliding through a dream, placing small rectangles of glossy paper on each table as he passed. A waiter, momentarily raised his head in the manner of a sleepy cat, surveyed the scene through narrowed bloodshot eyes then resumed his nap. I saw my distorted dual reflection reach out to take the paper from Mister Mirror Eyes, an unbidden snapshot for a psychedelic stereoscope, but he ignored me and put it on the table instead.

It was an advertisement, with a photo of a young woman wearing a helmet and a look of terror on her face. She had a man strapped to her back. He displayed his healthy gums in a wide-mouthed smile. The woman's mouth was open wide too, frozen in a silent scream that would have given goosebumps to Edvard Munch. Believe you can fly. Believe you can touch the sky, said the flyer. There was a smaller image of a parachute, and another with a small group of blonde tanned people, obviously representing the intended target audience, smiling with raised thumbs, presumably very pleased indeed to be back on solid ground. Perhaps they had never felt so alive. I imagined the exhilaration, the adrenaline coursing through their veins, heartbeats accelerating wildly as they stepped into the void.

The paper shook wildly in my hand. I put it back down on the table and surreptitiously checked out the Swedes instead. All four were broad-faced, with high sub-arctic cheekbones and unbrushed straw-blond hair, with the type of natural highlights that only came from prolonged exposure to sunlight and saltwater. They sat in silence, ignoring one another. Perhaps they had argued, or simply exhausted any useful conversation. Such things happen. Companionable silence, with a side-order of sultry sullenness and sunburn. One girl smoked, leaning back in her chair, chin tilted to the ceiling fan. She narrowed her eyes, hollowing her cheeks as she pulled strongly on the cigarette, then exhaled the smoke through her nose. I couldn't decide if the effect was sexy or disgusting. Or both. Her companions sat brooding, hunched over their phones, heads bowed as if in prayer, while Bob Dylan reassured everyone present that we didn't need a weatherman to know which way the wind blows. A yawing void opened up somewhere inside my chest. I caught my breath, teetering on the edge of the chasm that separated me from everything I had thought mere months earlier would be my future. After such a long time of unaccustomed abstinence my body longed for a woman, but my wounds were still too fresh and tender to be touched without unbearable pain. I looked for reassurance in the advertisement soaking in the condensation puddle from my beer glass, but found none there. It didn't fill me with an irrepressible thrill for life. It was just a flyer for falling.

It was Mrs Conway who suggested that I take a break away. I had dreaded the Dublin flat-hunting, the viewing of the cold damp hovels that would be all I could afford, and immediately gave in to her quirky logic. "Sure jaysiz, don't we owe you more than a month in overtime anyway, and ye haven't taken a day's holiday in god-only-knows how long. It'd give ye time to get yer head together, so it would. It's like Christy Moore says – everybody needs a break. That was a gas song now, so it was. D'ye remember it at all? Ah ye do."

There were two ferries to the island. I booked the morning one and shuffled aboard along with another hundred passengers. The air-conditioned cabin was as cold as a walk-in fridge and I felt my sweaty t-shirt cling uncomfortably as it cooled. Many of the locals, obviously used to the meat-locker conditions aboard, wore coats, or wrapped themselves in fleece blankets I recognised from Ikea, (was there no escape?) or more recently from news reports of refugees fleeing Syria. I reached into my backpack for a spare t-shirt and put it on, then wrapped another around my head like a turban.

A flat-screen TV at the front of the cabin showed a movie. There were loud explosions and screams and people getting shot or having their throats slit. A group of small children sat cross-legged on the carpet gazing up at the screen, entranced by the horrific carnage while their parents unpacked rice-based picnics that smelled strongly of fermented fish. There was no way to go out on deck, so I sat with my knees against the seat in front of me, hands tucked into my armpits for warmth. I lowered my chin to my chest and tried to sleep.

The crossing took almost two hours. By the sounds from the blaring television the death toll had been enormous. As I emerged from the floating refrigerated unit I was smothered by the heavy humid heat. I gave a taxi driver the name of a cheap guesthouse I had found online. Within minutes we were outside the sleepy little town clustered around the ferry port, passing rice paddies bordered with coconut palms and interspersed with ramshackle wooden houses where chickens and small children poked the ground in dusty yards shaded by huge tamarind and mango trees.

Traffic was light. Most of the vehicles we passed on the narrow roads were motorcycles, some driven by tourists, but most apparently on their way to or from the local school, three people or more astride the saddles, children dressed in neat school uniforms perched on the back, or squeezed between adults. Almost no one wore helmets. Other children walked along the dusty roadside, white school shirts glowing in the tropical light like an advertisement for detergent.

THE CLINIC WAS short-staffed and it wasn't hard to bluff my way into an unpaid job in exchange for board and lodgings. I took temperatures, held wrists and counted pulse rates, pumped blood pressure cuffs and watched the falling mercury, asked children to cough while placing a stethoscope on their backs – none of it was particularly complicated or hard to learn.

The clinic grounds consisted of a few single-story buildings clustered around a dusty courtyard, the soil a vibrant orange that matched the rusted corrugated roofs, the exact colour of Maria's hair in sunlight the time she dyed it with henna. I had my own room in one of the buildings. It was simple, just a camp bed and a mosquito net and a ceiling fan that I kept on all the time in a vain attempt to counter the ever-oppressive heat.

Apart from the other doctors, the real doctors, few of the clinic staff and almost none of the patients spoke English. I improvised my own sign language, communicating in a combination of mime and inquisitive and exaggerated facial expressions. A frown and a hand rubbed on my stomach expressed abdominal pain, a flourish of my hand dropped from my open mouth conveyed vomiting, a similar gesture below my lower back expressed something similar for the other end of the digestive tract, swivelling hands mimed bandage wrapping, forefingers made snipping scissors signs.

My white skin was an unearned badge of authority, my white lab coat a disguise, a suit of armour I wore at all times despite the heat, playing my role with the seriousness of a method actor. Despite my initial apprehension, it was disappointingly easy to deceive everyone. No one called my bluff. This confidence in my abilities, particularly from the local patients, was more than trust, it was reverential. I learned that they held their traditional healers and shamans in high esteem, but with a certain wariness, as they were also known for their ability to cast harmful spells. The western doctor was something more benign, yet not dissimilar. Though I rarely prescribed anything stronger than paracetamol, which people could have picked up themselves at the dispensary, it seemed important to them to receive the tablets from my hand, as if the medicine was an extension of the doctor, a physical manifestation of his magical powers.

I spent my free time online studying anatomy and the symptoms of common tropical ailments. There was so much to learn, the endless mysteries of the human body – in some ways so resilient, in others such a delicately balanced machine.

I settled into a routine. I thought I had finally found my calling. Most of the patients came to the day clinic. There was an unending supply of colicky babies whose cries called out like car alarms. Overweight and breathless women, wheezed bad breath and filled the out-patients waiting room with musky odours of stale sweat. I regularly saw diabetics with swollen feet and rotten toes who would have to make the trip to the mainland for amputation. It was a humbling atmosphere that made me grateful for many things that I had always taken for granted, robust health not the least of them. I reassured myself that despite my deceit my presence had a beneficial effect on these people's lives, but I knew that sincerity was no replacement for expertise and I lived in constant fear of being unmasked.

I had been sober for several weeks. During my waking hours I revelled in a newfound clarity, which I applied to my autodidactic medical studies, while at night I rediscovered a subconscious parallel universe of intense dreams that I had long forgotten. I spent sleepless hours analysing and dissecting the recurring scenes. I floated over Sweden, a country that I had never visited except in dreams, flying through pure fresh Scandinavian air over landscapes of clear water - streams, rivers, placid lakes - all bordered by forests of pristine pine. I woke up with the tangy dream smell of childhood Christmas trees still faintly lingering in my nostrils, the metallic taste of snow fading on my tongue. But more often I wasn't flying, I was falling, or just about to, teetering at an open door, looking down at clouds. There was a tiny moment, maybe just a fraction of a second, before I stepped into the void, a moment thinly sandwiched between the toasted rye bread slices of anticipation and exhilaration. There was a tiny death between the fear and the falling, before the ecstatic joy of surging adrenaline ripped me from headspace to meatspace and the thrill of being alive, not despite, but because of the danger.

I lay in the dark, hearing the night song of the cicadas and the frogs, trying to understand what subconscious drives lay behind this attempted annihilation of the self. What was I trying to gain? What was I trying to lose? In the dark awakedness of tropical night it became clear that it all lay in the single moment of abandonment, the casting off of previous narratives, a readiness to die to rise transformed like a flaming phoenix, or a butterfly tearing through the matrix of its chrysalis. But in the harsh light of day all these thoughts withered like the fallen jasmine flowers whose sweet perfume had been so seductive in the dark of night. The exhilaration of unfettered falling turned to fear as the ground sped faster towards me, becoming less abstract with each second that passed. Other nights I did not pass go, and went directly to jail, and woke, heart pounding, sweating in my cell. I tried to calm myself by listening to the fan chop the humid air into thick slices that were near impossible to breathe.

The novelty was wearing off. I was tired of being hot all the time. Apart from a couple of hours of pre-dawn coolness, that I usually slept through, there was no respite. The nearest air-conditioning was in the upscale cafés in the beach resorts dotted around the island's coast, but I stayed away. My budget was tight, but more importantly I couldn't risk being seen or recognised, even though I suspected this was probably giving disproportionate importance to the gravity of my crime. I wanted to leave but I couldn't. Every day I looked at the office calendar and saw the date of my return flight draw nearer. I would miss the flight, unable to travel on Dr Fintan's passport. If I contacted the embassy and told them my passport was lost it might lead to a visit from the police. I had no way of knowing if he had reported his passport stolen, or named me as the thief. What had seemed like an escape route had led me to a dead end. My island refuge had become a prison. I was trapped.

I was finishing my rounds when one of the nurses came running. A tourist had fallen off his motorbike. This was common enough. Between jellyfish stings and motorcycle accidents there was usually at least one foreign patient a day. Generally they weren't too badly bashed up, nothing worse than scraped knees or elbows. Calf muscles burned from hot tail pipes were all too common as well. But a few days earlier I had seen a girl – a young woman - who had broken her front teeth. I told her she needed a dentist, not a doctor. She told me she needed morphine. I slipped the needle into her arm as if I had been doing it my whole life, amazed that my hands didn't shake, all too aware that if I gave her too much she could slip into a coma or even die. The new arrival was in worse shape. A passing taxi had found him lying on the roadside, gathered him up and placed him in the back seat. Orderlies put the patient on a stretcher and carried him indoors.

He was unconscious. There was a nasty wound on his head but it had stopped bleeding. I checked his pulse while the nurse wiped away his mask of blood and dirt. He had shaved since I had seen him last. My hands shook as my fingers probed the lump swelling on the side of his head. Who knew what kind of damage was done to his brain? He might have amnesia, but I couldn't count on that. If he regained consciousness he would almost certainly recognise me and expose me for the fraud I was. There was still enough morphine in the dispensary to make sure that never happened. One of the nurses hooked him up to a glucose saline drip. It would be simple just to inject the morphine straight into the bag. In the meantime, there was nothing more that could be done. I told the nurses to call me if he regained consciousness and went back to my room where I looked up everything I could find to read about head injuries and concussions.

Dear Fintan. Dr Fintan. Only when I acknowledged the relief of his reappearance did I understand it as recognition of myself, of what I had abandoned. What was dear was not just Fintan, but my former self. Dear as in cherished, but also as in what it had cost to lose and find myself again.

What had caused me to take the decision based on an accident of fate? Was it the thrill of acting on impulse, abandoning myself, crossing a hitherto invisible or unimagined threshold? Or was it just a blind reaction, a survival instinct, like the drowning Swede reaching out to grab the nearest saviour? Floundering, I had latched on to Fintan, or his identity at least, and found myself caught up in a current that dragged me down another tributary, one I had never planned to explore. But now, even as he lay unconscious in the ward, Dr Fintan had unwittingly brought me splashing to the shore again, or close enough that I could wade. There was just one more thing I needed to do.

I waited until dark. I told the nurse on duty to take a break. Wooden slats near the high ceiling carved moonlight into diagonal sections. There were only two other patients in the ward and they were both asleep. I stealthily approached his bedside and stood watching him. He was breathing regularly. I bent over him, my heart pounding. I slowly pulled down the bed sheet and lifted his shirt, aware I was holding my breath. The money belt protruded just above the waistline of his jeans. I gently unzipped it, breathing a sigh of relief when my fingers found the passport. I checked his face, half-expecting to find him looking at me, but his eyes were still closed. His breathing hadn't changed. I removed the passport and replaced it with the original, zipped up the money belt and pulled the sheet back up over him. I took his hand in mine and whispered his name. His eyelids fluttered open.

"I called the embassy. They've contacted your family. How are you feeling?"

"Massive headache." His fingers explored the bandages wrapped around his head.

"How many fingers am I holding up?"

"One."

I knew that this and the fact that he could move were good signs.

"Listen, I have to go now. They'll look after you here, they're good people. Just take it easy."

"Where are you going?"

Off to a cold damp purgatory to pay penance for my sins, to see if I could build a new life from the ruins of the last. "I have a flight to catch."

"Oh." He blinked, turning his head to take in his surroundings. "What are you doing here anyway?"

Joget Girl

Evening sun buttered the alley in melted yellow light. Thick walls radiated the absorbed heat of the day. Johnny and Jamil sat with the other band members behind the theatre, upturned wooden Fraser & Neave drinks crates for seats, black bowties hung loosely at the unbuttoned necks of their matching shirts, cigarettes dangling from their fingers, or the corners of their mouths. The men talked lazily about nothing in particular, squinting as they sucked their cigarettes. None of them had yet reached their thirties. In contrast, Johnny's skin had lost the elasticity of youth. He noticed the finger's width of grey at the roots of his hair earlier in the mirror. The barber and his dye could wait another week.

A silhouette appeared at the far end of the alley. The younger men straightened up. One or two buttoned their shirts, tightening their bowties as the figure drew closer. They fell silent, aware of the even beat of her steps echoing in the evening stillness as her heels crunched over the rough paving and the gravel and the shards of glinting broken glass. A small white handbag dangled from the crook of her elbow. It swung from side to side with the rhythm of her steps. Her one-piece dress snugly hugged her curves. She wore dark glasses that curved upwards at the corners and gave her face a hint of feline. Her jet-black hair was piled high on her head in a bouffant beehive style, with bangs that curved down to meet her jaw.

She stopped beside the musicians. Blood-red nail polish flashed as she extracted a cigarette from her handbag. She inserted it into a sleek black cigarette holder as long and as fine as an artist's tapered paintbrush. Three sets of hands rose in simultaneous response. Each held a matchbox and a match. She let the bassist light her cigarette and inhaled sharply. When she exhaled, smoke streamed from her nostrils and her pouted full red lips. She took a few more draws on her cigarette, seemingly oblivious to the enraptured men. They gazed at her, bewitched, except for Johnny who studied his fingernails, a muscle in his jaw rhythmically clenching and unclenching. Ruby plucked the half-smoked cigarette from its holder and dropped it on the ground. A small curl of grey smoke rose from the still-smouldering butt. The men's eyes followed her as she walked towards the stage door. She pushed open the door and disappeared inside.

The trumpetist let out a low whistle. Others nodded silently.

"That Ruby sure isn't like the other girls," said the violinist, breaking the silence. There were chuckles and murmurs of agreement.

"You could say that again," said the bassist with a grin, theatrically wiping the sweat from his forehead.

The violinist bent down and retrieved the half-spent cigarette. He examined the lipstick stain, then put the cigarette in his mouth. "Sure tastes sweet."

"Closest you'll ever get to her lips."

"That makes two of us then."

"She acts like she doesn't care who knows who she is," said the accordionist.

"That's because she doesn't care. She's not an Ipoh girl. No one knows her here."

"They will, soon enough."

"Yeah, a beauty like that you don't forget too easily."

"She Chinese or Malay?"

"Where got Malay with such white skin one? Anyway, she speak Hokkien."

"Must be some kind of mix. Maybe even Sabah Sarawak."

"She don't talk like Sabah or Sarawak."

"I hear she has a room over at Mrs Tan's."

"Mrs Tan won't let her bring any fancy men back there."

"Who says she goes anywhere with fancy men? I've never seen her leave with anyone. All she does is dance."

"She's too young to go with a man anyhow."

"Too young? Who are you trying to fool? You mean you wouldn't?"

"How old is she anyway, seventeen?"

"Boss say she twenty-one."

"The boss says all the girls are twenty-one, the old ones and the young ones."

"What do you say, Uncle?"

Johnny had remained silent throughout, but now moved his gaze from his fingernails to his shoes.

"I say mind your own business. Leave the girl alone. I'm sure she has her reasons for being here, just like all of us. Anyway, it's about time we got started." He stood and held the stage door open and let the younger men file past.

THE PIANO HAD SEEN BETTER days, chipped ivory as nicotine yellowed as Johnny Chong's stained teeth. The dance hall, with its potted palms and art-deco architecture, was more home to him than the lonely room where he slept fitfully during the hottest hours of day, sweating in a Pagoda undershirt.

Johnny listened to the clink and clatter of cutlery and crockery, the percussive footsteps back and forth across the dance floor, the idle bass banter of the band members setting up, the complaining wheeze of an accordion removed from the red plush comfort of its case, the fizz of a match being struck. Cigarette smoke joined the smell of fried onions and chilli's acrid bite.

The waiters flapped out white tablecloths with a precise flick of their wrists, like fishermen casting nets - a sharp starched snap, followed by a moment of straight-armed silence as the white linen slowly glided down to drape the tables. Ceiling fans stirred a sea of swimming dust motes in the golden rhomboids carved from sunlight by the slatted openings near the roof.

Johnny cracked his knuckles and placed his gnarled fingers on the keys. The hall filled up with music, rapid florid arpeggios played in discordant keys.

The other band members exchanged glances. They smirked and sighed and slowly shook their heads. But Johnny didn't see, hear, or care.

He arrived early at the dance hall every evening to recreate the soundtrack of his youth; years of genteel evenings on cruise liners, with a girl in every port, when dancers waltzed to Brahms and Chopin, or danced the Charleston clear across the wide South China Sea.

Back in Tin-Town, Saint-Saens and Satie sustained him through soul-sapping nights of three-chord rumbas and local rhythms of ronggeng and joget.

Ruby popped her head into the kitchen, the cook more than happy to give her a bowl of rice and vegetables in exchange for fluttered eyelids and a cigarette. She pulled a chair over to the half-open door of the dressing room and listened to the piano while she ate, the music so unlike anything she had heard before, so different to the popular tunes she danced to with strangers every night. It was music you had to listen to, rather than hear. She smiled, recognising that she had never really understood there was a distinction. She closed her eyes and let the melodies weave a cocoon of discordant notes around her, hypnotising and transporting her to the inner reaches of her mind.

When she opened her eyes again she felt she had become someone else, someone more alive and present. She revelled in a strange sense of exhilaration that reminded her of breaking the rules when she was at the orphanage with the nuns, the excitement from the risk of getting caught more powerful than from anything she did.

The pianist intrigued her. He looked like any noodle-slurping Chinese uncle from the local kopitiam. She might pass him on the street and never guess the world he held inside, but he expressed things through music that made her learn things about herself, as if the music opened doors she didn't know were closed.

She finished her rice and used a piece of dampened charcoal to draw lines down the back of her calves in imitation of stocking seams. She added final touches to her mascara, applied lipstick to her pouted lips, hardly recognising the young woman in the mirror, transformed both outwardly and inwards.

One by one the other girls arrived. They slipped out of their plain street clothes and quickly dressed into kebayas and skirts. They applied makeup and frantically back-combed the blackness of their hair, adding wafts of hairspray to the floral scent of cheap perfume. None of them spoke to Ruby. She didn't expect or even want them to. They talked about her behind her back, but she didn't care. Was it her fault the men fell over themselves asking her to dance?

"WHAT WAS THAT, JC? MORE DEBUSSY?"

Jamil was the band's saxophonist, a quiet, large-handed man, the only one who ever really listened to Johnny when he played.

"Close, but no. Ravel."

"Sounded like Debussy to me."

"Easy to confuse them. At first."

The other band members were competent, talented even, but they lacked imagination, content to play within narrow musical horizons. Few had formal training, mostly they played by ear. Johnny was begrudgingly impressed at how they picked up a new tune after listening just two or three times to the record player. Their versions were never entirely accurate, and they couldn't resist adding a little local rhythm and flavour to the notes, but that was what the public loved. Anyway, who was he to judge? Music was borrowed across the artificial boundaries of nationality and culture. The popular songs they played, influenced by Arab musicians who played in the salons of Beirut and Alexandria, had in turn been borrowed from their Parisian counterparts, while Debussy's layered counterpoint bore the influences of gamelan.

Jamil was a musician's musician. Occasionally he played clarinet, but his obsession was the sax. Sometimes they sat together listening to jazz records from America, especially anything by a man Jamil called Bird. Jamil closed his eyes and moved his head in rhythm with the flow of notes. Johnny thought that he could hear what Bird was trying to get at, moving beyond the fixed strictures of scales to improvise new melodies that seemed to use every single note and half-note, shifting effortlessly between keys, boldly allowing himself absolute freedom of expression.

Jamil carefully slid the record back into its protective sleeve.

"The miracle of recording," he said, shaking his head with a smile. "Parker can play this over in New York and we can listen to it here in Ipoh."

"Yes, but soon we'll be out of a job," said Johnny. "Cheaper for a dancehall boss to pay for records instead of musicians."

"You worry too much. People want to dance to a live band. Dancing to music coming out of a machine just wouldn't be the same."

"I hope you're right."

SOME ARRIVED ON BICYCLES, most arrived on foot. The rich ones came in cars: Morris Minors, Rover P4s, even a Ford Deluxe Tudor. The main doors of the dancehall opened. In a flurry of excitement, customers poured in, laughing, talking loudly, waving cigarettes in exaggerated gestures, looking forward to an evening of musical entertainment, good food, and dance. Though the majority were men, there were women other than the joget girls. Couples, young and old, chatted animatedly, nodding or waving to their acquaintances. Some of the women wore jewellery: expensive-looking earrings, necklaces, bracelets. All wore wedding rings, even those who weren't married.

Other customers were more circumspect. They glanced around, unsure of themselves, stepping into this strange environment for the first time. Seeing these people who seemed so confident and self-assured only exaggerated their own insecurity. They ventured into the dancehall hesitantly, their wary eyes taking in the white-clothed tables, the candlelight reflecting on the glassware, the barmen in white jackets busy serving drinks and mixing cocktails. There was a stage at the end of the hall, where a group of musicians played in front of a long red pleated velvet curtain that reached up towards the dark and distant ceiling. Many of the customers made for the raised booths around the walls and huddled over candle-lit tables. A few occupied the tables set out on the edge of the dance floor, while others headed for the bar and ordered drinks. But the thing they noticed most, the reason they had come, was the line of women waiting to be asked to dance.

House rules said the girls couldn't refuse to dance with any man. The younger and the prettier girls were taken first. These nervous first-timers stood back, biding their time with fast-beating hearts, not knowing what to do with their hands, worried that when the time came to dance they would not know what to do with their feet.

Circumstances had made outcasts of some of the men: a man with pitted, pockmarked skin, another with a purple birthmark that poured down from his hairline and covered half his face, a man with a withered arm, love-hungry immigrants who saved their meagre earnings from the nearby Kinta Valley's tin mines. There were men who were uncommonly unhandsome, or unusually small. All were accustomed, but not inured to rejection from women, or never had the confidence or audacity to approach them in the first place. They savoured the knowledge that the dance tickets they clutched would guarantee them at least a few moments of female company.

Even though the joget girls came to the dancehall primarily to earn money it was also a diversion from the dull mundanity of quiet lives of poverty and desperation. There was money, excitement, affection, even adoration, things they had little experience of before, things they grew to enjoy, and even need.

Some of the men were clean and well-dressed, even handsome. When the girls were lucky they danced with men who charmed them and made them laugh, men who knew all the dance steps. But more often the men were clumsy and inept, trod on their toes, or slid their rough calloused hands from their lower backs down to their lower hips. Depending on the girl, and depending on the man, the hands were sternly redressed, or playfully slapped away, or maybe, maybe allowed to stay put. It was no secret that some of the girls left with the men. Some became mistresses and never returned to the dance hall, turning the page on this chapter of their lives without a second thought. Others met men on regular dates. Some of the joget girls had been known to break men's hearts, others had their own hearts broken.

Ruby promised herself never to cross that line. Sometimes she received gifts. Nothing extravagant, a new dress, a pair of shoes, makeup, a meal out, but it all added up. Those who could least afford it were the most generous. The rich ones were tightfisted, asked for free dances, or didn't want to pay for drinks, behaving as if they were entitled to things just because they wanted them. She supposed that was why they were rich. She took a page from their book and kept her expenses to the bare minimum, saving a little from her earnings every night. Mostly the men were well-behaved, but there were always those whose hands strayed after a drink or two. She kept them firmly in check. Occasionally they gave her money anyway, thinking she was playing hard to get, but in the end they found that she was true to her word. Some just shrugged and smiled, others cursed her beneath their breath.

There were Europeans among the crowd this evening, pink-faced school teachers with lacquered hair, planters on business taking a break from the social isolation of the rubber estates, and the inevitable British soldiers on leave, who thronged to these dancehalls, happier to drink and dance than hunt for communists in the highlands.

One of the soldiers asked Ruby to dance. The cloth of his uniform was rough under her hand and much too heavy for the climate. Her feet worked mechanically as her mind drifted away to other soldiers.

SHE WAS PLAYING under the green shade of a mango tree the afternoon the Japanese arrived. She huddled together with the other orphanage girls, anxiously watching the soldiers speaking with the nuns. One of the soldiers pointed towards the girls in the shade, long-limbed awkward girls whose adolescent bodies were blossoming towards womanhood.

The nuns shouted at the soldiers, beat their uniforms with their fists. The soldiers laughed and let the angry nuns push them into the refectory. One of the nuns reappeared a moment later. She called Ruby.

"Go to Mister Wong's and get two bottles of whiskey," she hissed. "Make sure he writes it down in the ledger." As if Mister Wong was likely to forget such a thing. "Bring one of the other girls with you and don't talk to anyone."

The nun had waited outside the refectory for their return. She took the bottles and shooed the girls away. A few hours later the merry soldiers left. That night, and many nights afterwards, the soldiers returned, but only a few at a time. Ruby and the other girls covered their ears trying to block out the nuns' screams and wails. They were old enough to understand what the soldiers were doing to the nuns. Ruby and the other girls prayed for the nuns, for the sacrifice they had made in order to protect them. Only years later did it occur to Ruby that the nuns' wailing might be anything other than screams of pain.

"The guys are all talking," said Jamil as they sat listening to a Lester Young record.

"Talking?" asked Johnny.

"About you."

"What about me?"

"We're not blind. You can't keep your eyes off her, can you?"

Johnny found himself blushing and at a loss for words. When he played he thought of himself as invisible, hidden by the protective wall built of musical notes.

"What are they saying?"

"That you're old enough to be her father. That you are human after all. That she knows you watch her. That you play piano just for her."

Johnny was embarrassed at being so transparent. He felt like a schoolboy caught misbehaving.

"You should ask her to dance. Get it out of your system. We can cover a few numbers without the piano. Give your fingers a rest and exercise your feet instead."

Johnny smiled weakly and quietly nodded. Anyone watching might have thought that he was rocking his head in time to the jazz record, but in fact he was making a silent agreement with himself.

Johnny waited a few nights, building up the courage. The musicians played on without him, grinning broadly as they watched him walk to the bar. He ordered a whiskey and downed half of it, then turned to face the dance floor. He leaned against the bar for support and watched her dance. For a moment their eyes locked, sealing an unspoken agreement. By the time the song had ended she had manoeuvred her dance partner close to the bar. At the final chord she slipped from her partner's grip and stood right in front of Johnny.

"You want to dance?" she asked, nodding at the tickets he clutched in his hand.

"That was supposed to be my line."

"So?"

"No, I don't want to dance. Can we sit down and talk?"

"Buy me a drink?"

"Sure."

"And a ticket per song," she said, delicately plucking a ticket from his hand.

Johnny nodded and tried to smile, but failed. "Let's sit."

He took her delicately by the elbow, a thrill of electricity running through his body at the moment of contact, and guided her to one of the empty booths.

"Well get talking, old man, you're halfway through your first ticket already."

She sat across from him, the candle casting flickering shadows over her face, the wavering flame reflected in her eyes, her lips slightly apart, hesitant, expectant, amused. It was almost too much to be this close to her. Under the table he wiped his palms on his thighs and silently chided himself for not taking a piss before asking her to sit down.

"Cigarette?" he asked, offering one extended from the pack.

She nodded and took it. She lit it straight off the candle, then leaned back and blew smoke into the air, where it joined the blue-grey pall that softened the outlines of the evening. Johnny lit his own cigarette and watched the busy waiters pass back and forth, wheeling trolleys, balancing trays of glasses, carrying plates. The music was accompanied by the hum of conversation, the scrapes of chairs being moved, the erratic percussion of cutlery on crockery and clinked glasses raised in toasts.

"I never thought it sounded like this," he said after a moment. "Up there on the stage, you are in the music, surrounded by it. You are the music. Down here it's like the music is in the background."

Another song came to an end. "They play pretty good without me," he said, passing her another ticket and placing another on the table to reserve the next dance as well.

"It only sounds different because there's no piano, that's all. When I'm dancing the music is all there is for me as well. Just me and the music, turning round and round."

"What about the men you dance with?"

"What about them?"

"Well aren't they there with you?"

"Oh, they're there with me alright, but I'm not there with them. Never have been, never will be." She took another long drag on the cigarette, narrowing her eyes against the smoke.

"You don't have your cigarette holder tonight?"

"It puts things at a distance. Sometimes I like to bring things a little closer."

Johnny nodded as if he understood, but in truth he didn't know what she meant. Maybe she didn't mean anything.

"You like to watch me dance, don't you?"

Her smile was ambiguous. Was she mocking him? It was a smile that didn't seem to reach her eyes. Or maybe it was the effect of the reflected candle flames in her dark pupils.

"Yes," he said. "Yes, I like to watch you dance. I like to look at you. You are very beautiful."

She inclined her head in a slight bow of acknowledgement. Johnny felt the blood rush to his face. He swallowed a mouthful of whiskey and winced as it seared down his throat. He tried to pass it off as a smile. He coughed.

"Where were you before you came to Ipoh?"

"Nowhere."

"Everyone is from somewhere. Where did you grow up? Where is your family?"

"I don't have a family. My mother put me in an orphanage so that I wouldn't starve. The nuns took care of me."

"You know you ..." He looked around at a loss for words, drawing in his lips.

A slight frown crossed her face. She leaned forward and gave him a nod of encouragement.

"What I want to say," he said. "What I really want to say ..."

Her elbows were on the table. The ash on the cigarette between her fingers curved downwards, threatening to drop off. He looked from the cigarette to her face and took a deep shuddering breath.

"You look just like your mother. When she was your age."

"My mother? What do you know about my mother?" she asked warily.

"She was the most beautiful woman in Johor. You're from Johor originally, isn't it?"

Ruby leaned away from the table, wedging herself into the corner between the high-backed seat and the wall. The composed young woman became the vulnerable orphan she tried to hide.

Johnny was aware of movement under the table as she crossed her legs. He took out his wallet and carefully unfolded a creased black and white photo. He handed it to Ruby reverentially, as if offering joss sticks at an altar.

"Do you recognise her?"

Ruby fixed her eyes on the photo. She nodded slowly, slid the photo back across the table and folded her arms.

"How is she? Do you see her? Does she know you are here in Tin-Town?"

"She stopped visiting me at the orphanage when the Japanese came. After they left I thought she might come back, but she never did."

"They killed her?"

"I don't know. So many died."

"Did she ever mention me?"

The music stopped. There was a moment of movement while the other joget girls changed partners. Another song began. Johnny slid the third ticket across the table and placed another in front of him. She took the ticket and looked anxiously over her shoulder, unsure of who or what she was looking for.

"She mentioned something about a man who played piano. I never thought that it was you."

"What did she say about this man who played the piano?"

"That he was no good. That he had ruined her life. That he had taken her from her family and then abandoned her and her baby, disgraced her, and finally left her penniless with nowhere to live. She thought he might come back, but he never did. She said all men are the same, that they never should be trusted, that she never should have been so stupid as to fall in love."

Johnny swallowed. He waved down a waiter and ordered two more drinks.

"I'm sorry," he said, after sipping on the whiskey. "I wasn't a very good husband. I suppose I was an even worse father."

Her lower lip quivered. Even though the song wasn't over she snatched the ticket from the table and stood.

"You were never a father to me. You never will be."

She turned and walked across the dance floor, elbowing her way through the dancers. Johnny let her go without a word and watched her disappear behind the dancers, towards the dressing rooms, his fingers worrying the last ticket, the ticket he would never use.

The night drew to a close. The band played the final dance, the dancers moved apart. Johnny sat watching the dying candles as one by one the flickering flames went out.

The musicians sat on upturned wooden crates, smoking in the lemony light.

“She found herself a fancy man. She was never going to stay here long.”

“I bet you’re right. A girl with looks like that could have her pick of any man.”

“She never seemed like the settling type to me. She’ll be dancing somewhere else by now, maybe Penang, or Alor Setar. Maybe even Singapore.”

“I think old Uncle Johnny here frightened her away, that right, Johnny?” The men laughed at the unlikelihood.

“Uncle? How come you never play early anymore?”

“Finally decided to stop torturing us with that crazy music?”

Johnny winced as he drew the last smoke from the cigarette clenched between his yellowed fingers, dropped the butt on the ground, and ground it with his shoe. He raised his head and looked towards the end of the alley, waiting for her silhouette to reappear in the cloud of exhaled smoke.

Heliotrope

She lies angled like a solar panel, optimally tilted for maximum absorption, though she supposes she'd get just as much exposure lying flat on her back, wouldn't she? But being supine would make it harder to look around, and she wants to look around. People watch. She holds her head straight, as if gazing wistfully out towards the horizon beyond the big noisy slushy waves, while her eyes roam behind the huge sunglasses she's decided to wear this season, shielding all that delicate skin around her eyes from those harmful UV rays, even though there's already a lattice of fine wrinkles there that betrays her age. The glasses cost a packet, not that she minds paying for quality, trusting, or not quite trusting, but hoping, giving the benefit of the doubt, that a premium brand would really use the UV glass they promised.

She takes in the bodies, some of them as immobile as her own, shielded by parasols or sprawled full sizzle on beach towels, skin ashine and glossy with overpriced creams and oils and sprays. Children dig with plastic shovels in the firmer sand near the water's edge. Young couples splash and squeal and laugh, bouncing as the waves crash against their lithe fit bodies. Older couples stroll, sometimes hand in hand, more often not, heads lowered, occasionally stooping to gather seashells. Older men with grey-furred torsos wear knee-length shorts or trousers rolled, walking with their hands clasped behind their backs, sometimes stopping to look out to sea and incidentally take in the view of young women whose wave-bashed bikini bottoms have ridden up between their butt cheeks. Or maybe the swimwear is designed that way. It's hard to tell at this distance. Some people wear hats. More wear sunglasses. Bodies of all shapes and sizes and ages. There's something reassuringly democratic about the lack of clothes as social markers. Still there's a certain poise or rigidity, or an ease or fluidity in people's movements that betray their feelings about themselves. Teenage girls with hunched shoulders. Gangly boys who haven't yet grown into their long limbs.

At this angle, this solar-panelled angle, she can read, or could read if she could be bothered, which it turns out she isn't, the paperback she picked up at the airport on the way here, still unopened in her beach bag. Then there's that thing about sounds, the way you can never really tell for sure what direction they are coming from when you lie down flat. She can do without that kind of disorientation, thank you very much. So, tilted it is, angled like a ... Over the length of the afternoon she'll move the bench around. Though it's not called a bench, is it? What's the word, a lounger? That doesn't sound right either, more a word to describe a layabout, a scrounger, someone who frequents noisy smoky bar lounges. Of course there's no smoking in bars these days, hasn't been for a while now, a good few years, which is a plus. Just drink yourself to death instead of smoke and drink yourself to death. Save your lungs and ruin your liver anyway. Not much of an improvement, is it? Or maybe it is. Must be awful being short of breath, clothes and hair always stinking. That liquid cough from tar-filled lungs her grandfather used to do. Pack a day since he was nine years old. There was only one way that was ever going to end.

In a minute now she'll shift and readjust this bench, this layabout. No, that's still not the right word. Turning in the sun, still like a solar panel, one of those automated ones that somehow knows how to track the sun, the way a newborn follows its mother's eyes. Heliocentric. No, not heliocentric. Heliotropic, like sunflowers. What is it the Spanish call them? Girasol? Or is that Italian? Anyway, at least her vocabulary hasn't totally forsaken her. She remembers that the 'gira' part is related to gyration and gyroscope, and even those Greek gyros kebabs, the huge lumps of meat twisting slowly on their skewers to get evenly cooked. Speaking of which, she'll have to give her back a blast and give her front a rest. Funny to think that sunflowers and kebabs could have anything in common. What goes around comes around, as they say. Wheels on the bus. It's all about heat and rotation. Rotation and radiation. The flower stalk, the metal skewer, the axle on which the whole great world spins. Is it axle? No, axis, that's it, pronounced similar to access but with limited centripetal reach. Girasol though, good word that. Where on earth did she even dig it up from? One of those unknown knowns. Didn't even know she knew it until she did. Same 'sol' as parasol too, isn't it? Like the big red one standing folded at her side, though plenty of others have theirs open, throwing shade, lounging around on their layabouts, their lounge-boys. No, that's not it. What the hell is this bloody bench actually called? All these words, but not the only one she needs. Well, not needs, but wants. Wasn't it Jagger said something similar once? The problems of half of humanity there in a phrase.

Mind you, she could patent them as brand names. Was a time, if you got in early enough, you could have registered the names and bought the internet domains. Domains. Always sounds so grand, a country estate or a vineyard, not just a string of letters that some company might want to use sooner or later – LOUNGEBOY.COM, LAYABOUT.COM – sell them on for a tidy profit, though you'd probably need better names than those.

Now her arm is in the shade of her neighbour's parasol. That won't do. There's no more putting it off. She'll have to stand up, undo the ratchet and shift the bench around so that she's still in alignment with the sun. Then she can lie flat on her front and undo her straps so she doesn't end up with tan marks. Careful not to fall asleep, forget she's no longer tied in, so to speak, sit up and expose herself to all and sundry the way younger women used to without a second thought but don't seem to anymore.

It's funny how things shift, the fashions, though it's more than a fashion, isn't it? The social norms you could call it. Mores. Or is it pronounced 'moray'? When the moon hits your eye ... Ouch. That's the thing with learning words through reading that you never hear people use in real life. Maybe she needs new friends, friends with broader vocabularies. Or a better class of podcasts. But the whole topless thing. One minute it's perfectly fine to let everything hang out, if that's what you decide to do. Next thing you know women won't even dare breastfeed their babies in public for fear of being shouted out of it by some random puritan who can't mind his own business. Because it's always a 'him', isn't it? A 'he'. A 'his'. Or worried some perv will snap photos and post them online. That's what the world has come to. A woman's body is no longer her own. Though was it ever? Not when you consider that it could be temporarily occupied by your future offspring. She's had a few tenants herself. Three. Or four if you count the one that didn't make it. Even after all this time, decades now, she still hasn't really gotten over that. Doubts she ever really will. Or even wants to for that matter.

Two lives sharing the same body. How peculiar is that? The miracle of life. Maybe that's what makes men so greedy. They never have to share their bodies with another person, or a series of persons, never have to make the compromises needed to ensure the future of humanity. Maybe she's onto something there, the root of all that's wrong with the world. Or half of it anyway.

Now she really needs to turn over and stop just thinking about it. And on second thoughts she probably won't bother unstrapping herself at all. At her age she should be past caring about tan lines on her back that only a few people will ever see, none of them being herself. So odd that other people can be more familiar with our backs than we ever are ourselves, even though they've been ours our whole life long.

She twists and places both feet firmly on the ground and sits up straight, back vertical, no longer solar panel angled. She gives herself a moment for the blood to sink towards her feet, so she doesn't come over all dizzy when she stands up. She thinks again, searching for the word for this contraption, this layabout, this scrounger, and wonders if losing your words is a sign of something more serious. Maybe it's normal for her age. Or it could be the heat has her brain addled, stewed in a brain pan, poached. Or maybe it's just that you more easily retain the vocabulary you actually need and use. Whatever the word is for this bench she'd only need it for one week a year. And every year she won't learn the local word, wherever she happens to be, never mind the word in English, if one even exists.

Heliotrope. She's surprised she remembered that one, unsure of where she learned it, or even if she's ever said the word aloud. Maybe that's what she'll call this bench – a heliotrope. Better than layabout or lounge boy anyway. Patent the brand name, buy the domain, HELIOTROPE.COM, if it's not already taken. Probably is, but still. She should look into what technology those sun-tracking solar panels use. Maybe it's just as simple as a timer calibrated against the hours of sunrise and sunset. She could invent a solar-tracking lounge boy, a gyrating layabout, a heliotropic scrounger. Would there even be a market for that kind of thing? Make it expensive, a luxury product. Must be enough squillionaires out there with less sense than money, fans of automation who would buy it, use it as a toy, maybe just once, before they discard it like those treadmills or cycling machines people buy and never use. Mind you they've come back in fashion again, haven't they? Call it re-cycling. What goes around comes around. Spinning - all the way to the top. Could patent a slogan like that. All that effort to end up exactly where you started. A more accurate slogan. But the heliotrope, all the resources it would needlessly use. The more she thinks about it the worse the idea seems.

Still, at least she knows what to call the bloody thing now, even if it's not the real name, even if no one would know what she was on about if she was to say it out loud. Besides, she's never been an inventor. Not to say she couldn't have been, given a different life and different doors and opportunities. Anyone could. Or maybe not anyone. Some definitely wouldn't be cut out for it, even with all the golden opportunities laid out on silver platters and served up with silver spoons. Anyway, that's all well and good, but she's even more in the shade now. And she should really lie down on her heliotrope again, close her eyes and turn her back on it all, the sun, the bathers, the swimmers, the diggers, the splashers, the strollers, the readers, the sleepers, the ice cream cones and frisbees. The gulls. The roar of the surf. The heliotrope.

Transect

I did the sit, tuck, and twist that lifted my legs into the hammock, zipped the net and clicked on the flashlight. It had to be in that order. Putting the light on before closing the net meant sleepless nights and new additions to my already impressive collection of mosquito bites. I checked every fold of my nocturnal cocoon for intruders, swallowed a dose of larium, and clicked off the light. Squirming into my sleeping bag I hung swaying, disorientated and pendulous, night-blind. Insects whined and buzz-sawed through the dark. High in the canopy night birds broadcast their opinions, echoed moments later by distant refutations, back and forth with monotonous regularity – oh yes you did, oh no I didn't, did, didn't, oh yes you did, oh no I didn't …

It had been a long day, the fourth since I let Mr Azman go. His daily stipend, though meagre, had strained my limited financial resources, but without him I was spending more than twice as long measuring quadrants and hammering in stakes. I swung, second-guessing myself, wondering if economies of scale could have justified the extra cost. Hiking back out to find him would cost me at least another full day. And another back in. Two days lost right there. I didn't have that kind of time to lose.

Months earlier I had placed a wooden ruler on a map, my path defined with one swift swipe of a pencil. The transect cut shore to shore across the remotest part of the island. It looked easy on paper, but nothing is simple in the tropics.

The next day started as days generally do, the sun rising somewhere above and beyond the trees, gradually dispelling the ground mist that had gathered in the cool hours just before dawn. I lit a small fire of twigs and leaves, just enough to cook porridge and heat water for tea. I spent a few minutes whetting the edge of Mr Azman's parang. The mass of the mountains lurked unseen nearby. My path skirted their foot, but avoided any steep climb. I folded camp, a simple operation that entailed untying my hammock and stuffing it, sleeping bag and all, into my backpack. Following my compass I counted my steps, my voice strangely misplaced in this environment, but if I didn't count out loud my mind wandered up lianas, hid in the mossy alcoves of buttress roots, followed flittering butterflies and tiny military trails of ants. Then I ended up retracing my steps to the previous quadrant and starting again.

Sweat leaked through my forehead, draining directly from my heat-befuddled brain. Every hundred steps I stopped, shrugged off my pack, and searched for saplings to cut into stakes. I catalogued species a square metre at a time, peering through a sweat-smudged magnifying glass, balancing a notebook on my knee, my back aching each time I stooped or stood. I wrote down everything I knew and made passable sketches of the things I didn't. (17 x insects, 1 scorpion, shaded, dead leaves, rattan palm.)

Leaves rustled overhead. I froze, alert, my mouth open. Dark shapes in the trees resolved themselves into a troop of spectacled langurs. The white rings around their eyes gave them a look of permanent surprise. They watched me watching them, and seeing that I didn't seem to pose a threat, returned to their leisurely browsing, stripping leaves from their stems.

My initial plan had been to just specifically study these

monkeys for my dissertation. Though closely related to other species on the mainland, they were unique and only found on this island. As I planned my trip I wondered how they got here. The mainland was too distant for them to have swum across, and even floating on a storm-felled tree, or a raft of vegetation, over that distance seemed unlikely. I suspected that they had been deliberately introduced. My favoured origin theory included them being escaped pirates' pets. Or perhaps people from the mainland had exiled them here in order to protect their crops and orchards. But these ideas didn't hold up much to scrutiny. Given the size of the island an escaped pet or two would be unlikely to give rise to an extensive population, and if they had become pests on the mainland it would have been easier to hunt and kill them than trap them and set out on a long sea journey. I decided studying the langurs in their natural habitat could provide further clues to their origins. I would learn everything there was to know about them and become a leading world expert, famous for having solved the mystery of the island's langurs. Then it occurred to me to look at the geological record. An afternoon in the library gave me the answer I was looking for. Being equatorial, during the Last Glacial Maximum the seas hadn't frozen, but had diminished enough to create a landbridge between the island and the mainland. The intervening 20,000 years since the seas rose again gave ample time for an isolated pocket of monkeys to continue their evolutionary path, adapting to the microcosm of the island's biotope. I wondered if the local human population had also been stranded here as the icecaps retreated and sea levels started to climb, but those were questions best left to anthropologists. Given that I had more or less solved the mystery of their origin without even leaving the campus I needed to look at other themes for a field trip. Since I already had my sights set on the island I decided to cast my net wider and examine if the same evolutionary motors of time and isolation had led to any other endemic variations among the island's fauna and flora.

I had completed modules in tropical botany and entomology, but these were cursory at best and almost everything I found was unfamiliar. Looking through my magnifying glass I was confronted with the fact that I didn't really know what I was looking at. There were hundreds of types of trees alone, many with leaves only at the crown, high in the canopy, difficult to make out even with binoculars. I noted everything scrupulously, determined to compare my findings with existing records on my return.

Nature adores symmetry, but she also abhors straight lines, yet in a near-infinite variety of possibilities even the most unlikely things occur. A week after Mr Azman left I started to notice unusual leaves on the forest floor. Some fell within my quadrants, most didn't. What made these leaves noteworthy was that they were almost perfectly rectangular.

I had no idea whether they started out that shape directly from the bud, or gradually distended as they grew. I could think of no natural advantage offered by such a variation, but in evolution random mutations that don't offer any particular disadvantage can get passed on as well, and in a restrained environment and population even a small variation can have big repercussions over time.

Though I still wasn't sure what type of tree produced these leaves, by observing the bark and roots of trees nearby I had narrowed down the likely candidates. Most of the leaves were about a foot long. I was almost certain that I would have come across them in my studies if they were known. What a coup it would be to discover an entirely new species of tree. It might even be named after me.

Though dry, the leaves were remarkably supple and resilient, their inner veining so faint that the surface was almost smooth, and unlike the russets and reds of other fallen leaves, these were very pale in colour. I had no idea what they looked like on the trees, but I imagined that they must have been pale green. Though I had decided that I wouldn't burden myself by collecting and carrying many samples, I started to gather these leaves.

I hung suspended in my nocturnal chrysalis, sweating and shivering. Malarial prophylactics don't offer immunity or protection and the previous days were spent in blurred stumblings and blinding headaches that were probably caused as much by dehydration as by the parasitic protozoa wriggling their way through my bloodstream. Through the roaring fog of fever I had a brief moment of lucidity and awareness. It was preternaturally quiet, the birds making their absence felt through their sudden silence. A simian whoop from somewhere in the canopy was answered almost instantly. These calls in turn received replies, so that soon the noise grew into a collective cacophonous crescendo that suddenly stopped cold. The subsequent silence was broken by the ping of a small bell. Then another, and another. Soon the forest was alive with the sound of tiny bells. As I listened, disorientated, but intrigued, I became aware of a rhythmic tap, tap, clap. The sound continued all through the night, insinuating itself into fever dreams of rain falling on tin roofs, horses clopping over cobblestones, dry wood crackling in a fireplace, popcorn exploding, footsteps hurrying down endless flights of stairs. All this was punctuated with pings from the mysterious tiny bells.

I prised my eyes open and looked around the dappled morning light of the clearing where I had camped. The larium gave me heartburn and a hangover, but the fever had finally broken. I remembered tiny bells from my dreams. I slept again, dreaming I was a cockroach. I didn't fumble on my back in bed waving my six legs in the air, no, not I. I was wise in the ways of the cockroach and was one of them, their own size and shape. I'd like to say that being a cockroach intrigued me, but in fact I was terribly bored. I wanted to revert back to my human form. The elder cockroach admonished me sternly. "Why do you want to go with them? Are you not our brother? They are a doomed species.

They will die out and be no more. This is nature, the huge circles it makes, evolution and extinction. Their time is now, but shall not be forever. And when they are gone who shall remain? Us brother. You are one of our kind, stay with us, stay with us, stay with us..."

I woke up with a jolt. A monkey crouched on the other side of the netting. He sported a grey goatee and mane and seemed to be blind in one eye while the other was badly bloodshot. He looked tired and held himself in the way of one entrusted with a distasteful task, doing his duty against his own personal inclination. He clutched a ream of page leaves to his chest, grunted once and gently placed them on the ground, then fixing me with his one half-good eye, stared at me for an impolite length of time before shuffling off into the undergrowth. I unzipped the net, swung out of my hammock and picked up the pile of page leaves he had left.

I almost tripped over the first typewriter. It was hidden under a pile of leaves and half-covered with rust and moss. As I counted out my steps to the next quadrant I saw more of them. I stopped counting. There were typewriters everywhere. Typewriters in the bushes, typewriters balancing on rocks, typewriters half-buried in anthills, lodged in the crooks of trees, submerged in meandering streams that crisscrossed the jungle floor. High up in the tree tops, hidden among the leaves, monkeys randomly clattered at the keys. Occasionally a typewriter was casually chucked from above, landing with a smash on the forest floor, joining the other wrecks that lay among the dead leaves, fallen branches and ubiquitous ferns. In fact most of the typewriters I saw were broken. I witnessed one belligerent monkey smashing a typewriter with a rock, venting his rage at these machines and their meaningless symbols that had somehow invaded his life.

My transect forgotten, I wandered through this landscape, watching monkeys rolling page leaves into typewriters, hammering keys, reproducing the sounds from my dreams. Whenever they reached the end of a line there was a little pinging bell. The monkeys ignored me. I tried to read what they were writing, but of course, apart from a random word or two that they had managed to produce by chance, it was all just gibberish, except for the pages the cycloptic elder had given me, the ones you've just finished reading.

Obedient Wife

She's having trouble growing up. It's not her fault. Anyone in her situation would face similar issues. Her father is a strict authoritarian. His anger is unpredictable. Every time she tries to spread her wings he reaches for shears to clip them. He has so many rules, spoken and unspoken. She cannot speak up. Most of the time she isn't sure what it is she wants to say. How to translate feelings and thoughts into words? As she feels his shears snip through her feathers her father screams at her to be grateful.

Her mother ... her mother is many things. Most of the things her mother is she keeps hidden, from her daughter, from herself. If her mother was allowed to open up and blossom into the woman she knows she can be, or could have been, it would be less a flowering than an act of destruction. Her mother thinks about smashing all the dishes in the kitchen. Her mother thinks about taking the knife she uses for killing chickens and using it on her husband's neck instead, his thick warm blood oozing over her fingers. Later her mother feels guilty for fantasising about these things. Her mother lives in fear. Fear of her husband. Fear of what might happen in this life. Fear of what might happen in the next. She shows her affection for her daughter through food. Everyone agrees her mother is an excellent cook.

Lately, her daughter has noticed that her mother cooks with cheaper ingredients. The fish and meat and seafood they used to eat almost every day are reserved for special occasions now. The chickens are more valuable for their eggs than for their meat. She eats the cheap broken rice her father brings home and the kangkung he insists they eat. The daughter watches her mother laugh. She laughs only with her mouth. Her mother's eyes never lose their sadness. The daughter wonders if this is who she will become, if this is all she will ever be allowed to become. A woman like her mother. An obedient wife.

Majestic Heights

He watches her every morning from the eighth floor, leaning elbows on the low parapet wall outside his apartment. He doesn't know her name and he has hardly ever seen her face, but it's always her that his homesick eyes seek out. She walks across the car park, out onto the road and joins the other women waiting for the bus. They all wear the same blue uniforms and white tudungs, but there's something about the confidence she exudes that draws his eye to her, the poise that contrasts with the other women's slouched resignation. He wills her to turn around and look up at him, but a small convoy of blue buses arrives and she's lost in one of the huddles of identically dressed young women who climb aboard.

After the buses leave he goes indoors. His feet are sore and his tired legs ache after another long night at the restaurant. He hardly even has the energy to eat the food he has taken home, but somehow manages to shovel the half-cold rice into his mouth. He throws the greasy Styrofoam container in the bin along with all the others, disturbing the cockroaches who claim the mouldy kitchen as their domain.

He shares the tiny bedroom with three colleagues. They all come from Nepal. They live together and yet he always has the apartment to himself. The other three work the day shift. He only sees them arriving at the restaurant in the morning just before he leaves and again at night when it's time to start his shift.

He puts his shirt and folded trousers on a hanger and hooks it on a nail protruding from the flaking paint of the half-rotten wooden window frame. He'll get one more shift out of these clothes before he has to scrub them clean. He climbs up to the upper bunk and lies there with the ceiling at arm's length, seeing clouded patterns in the damp stains, still thinking of the girl. He wonders what sort of work she does and where the blue buses go. The rumbling lullaby of morning traffic lulls him off to sleep.

Forty white tudungs are multiplied in reflection in the bus windows. She sees her own image superimposed on the morning traffic. This uniform was once the mark of status, it meant she was someone who had a job, but now she hates it and the way it robs her individuality. She pulls her phone out of her handbag and texts in Bahasa Indonesia to her mother in Medan, asking if she received the money she sent for Aminah's school uniform. Her baby is starting school today. How did that happen so fast? She slowly blinks and swallows back the lump in her throat. Her exhaled breath is shaky as she presses 'send'.

At the factory she finds her usual spot and settles down for the next twelve mind-numbing hours soldering components to a motherboard. Mother bored. She half snorts at her own joke, but doesn't smile. She's been learning English since she came to this country. It might help her get a supervisor's job.

She works a six-day week. The only break is lunchtime, and for those who want, there's time to pray. She has to wear glasses now while she works. Her job is robbing her of her eyesight. She knows she should be wearing some protective mask against the noxious fumes that make her dizzy, but there are no rules or special precautions in this place. No one dares complain for fear of losing their jobs. She knows how easily any of the factory workers are disposable, interchangeable, and can be replaced.

The monotony of her job allows her mind to run free. She runs through the plots of the Indonesian television dramas she and her friends watch at night. They have become her new family in this country— her flatmates and the characters on the television with their stories of romance.

Her mind drifts towards the boy - the one she sees every morning up high on the building next to hers. He looks so lost and lonely. She knows just how he feels. Sometimes she's sure he's watching her, though why should he pay any attention to her? Maybe it's her imagination. She wonders where he's from. It must be somewhere other than this country. As far as she can tell only foreign workers live in Majestic Heights.

HE LEANS on the low wall and watches her pass below. He wills her to turn around and look up at him. It's not too much to ask, just a little glance, some sort of acknowledgement to show that she knows that he exists. And then what? He longs for someone to break his loneliness. His body cries out to be touched. He feels a throbbing ache across his chest. He has never touched a woman, he has never had a kiss. Her bus comes as it does every morning and then she's gone again.

HE SCRUBS his clothes clean on the rough cement bathroom floor, wearing just his underwear. He rinses the soapy clothes in a bucket and shakes them out. The fabric makes snapping sounds and sends cooling water droplets splashing over his near-naked body. He places the clothes neatly on the hanger and hangs them at the window in the bedroom. By evening time they will be dry.

She feels his eyes on her. She can't say how, but she feels his lonely longing tingle on the back of her neck. She knows if she looks around he will be watching. Instead she keeps her eyes cast towards the ground.

On the bus the girl sitting next to her is also from Medan. The girl talks about her family, about how when she has saved enough she will go back home and open a small shop. She's not in a rush to find a husband. This girl wants to be independent.

She listens to the girl and mentions nothing of her own husband, how she was married at sixteen. How she gave birth five months later. She keeps silent about the way that he beat her and shouted at her, before she finally got away. Her mother says that he is gone now, but she's afraid that he will find her when she manages to return. In the meantime the best she can do is save as much money as possible so that her mother can look after her baby girl.

The rain pours down outside and wet customers hurry in, sheltering their heads with newspapers, umbrellas, or even with their hands. Though it isn't cold, some gather in a huddle next to the tandoor, hoping the scalding heat will dry their clothes. For some reason it's busy tonight and everybody orders naan. It's always like that. Someone orders first and the yeasty smell of the fresh bread fills the restaurant, bringing water to everybody's mouths. Then they all decide that they want naan as well.

He likes to knead the uncooked dough and feel its texture in his hands. He keeps at it until his forearms ache.

He and his colleagues enjoy a rough fraternal physicality together. They massage each other's shoulders, or playfully thump each other on the arms. Occasionally they hug. Sometimes they even hold hands, but the customers look at them strangely when they do that. The people in this country never seem to touch.

He wonders what it would be like to massage the factory girl's shoulders. Would her flesh be strong and meaty like his colleagues? He kneads the dough more delicately now, imagining he's touching her. He smiles as he places the naan inside the hot tandoor.

He yelps as his hand touches the inside of the oven. He shakes his hand in pain. He knows he should do something about it, but there are still too many orders.

By the end of the shift he has a nasty blister on the outside edge of his hand. One of his colleagues wraps his hand with cotton wool and gauze from the restaurant's first-aid kit.

Just after dawn he walks back home. The lift is out of order again. He's still out of breath from climbing up eight flights when he sees her walking past. He wills his breath to slow down and concentrates on the girl. Please just look. Let me know that you know that I am here.

His eyes are on her again. She knows she shouldn't, but she has to check to make sure it's true. She turns her head.

Their eyes meet.

SHE HOLDS his gaze for a second or two and then she turns away, smiling softly to herself.

Somehow it feels good to be seen. She's reassured that it wasn't just her imagination. Though their eyes only met for just a moment, his face stays with her for the rest of the day. She sees him in the wisps of smoke writhing from the melting solder.

She flinches as her hand brushes against the hot soldering iron. Now she has a nasty burn.

She looked. She saw me.

He can't suppress his smile. If there had been someone else at home he would tell them, though they would probably laugh at him. Still, he is happy. He feels vindicated. This was proof that they had an invisible connection. They had established contact of a sort. He was still smiling as he lay down on the bed, seeing her face in the patterns of damp stains up on the ceiling.

He doesn't climb the stairs. He waits in the parking lot under the cool morning shade of the tacoma trees, the pink blossoms exuberant, surprising in trees that are so unremarkable for most of the year. Had twelve months already passed since he had last seen them bloom? Yet it seemed so long ago. How to make sense of the passage of time in this place where the weather was the same stifling heat every day of the year, when the length of day varied from the longest to the shortest by only a few minutes? The only seasons here were indoors and outdoors, the only respite in the coolness of the air-conditioned shopping malls. He envied his compatriots who worked there, while he spent his nights sweating over a hot tandoor.

The girls in uniform pass him by. Some chatter in tight huddles, their steps falling in unison. Others walk alone, their eyes cast down towards the ground.

Then he sees her.

She is delicate and slender, though her face is pitted with acne scars.

Their eyes meet. He smiles nervously at her. She stares back at him for a beat too long, before she turns her head away. There's something in the deliberate defiance of that gesture that makes her seem strong and even more attractive to him. Her face was unreadable. Impassive.

He sees the bandage on her hand and smiles again, lifting his hand to show his own wrapped burn. She tries to hide her smile, but it pulls at the corners of her mouth. He is quite handsome. He is strong and stocky, though he is not very tall. They stand close together. Neither says a word. Then the shuffling of feet and the rumbling of the blue buses break the spell and she turns away to leave for work.

He flies up the stairs, his face a broad grin the whole way up the eight floors. He is too excited to sleep. He lies on the bed and tries to picture what lies beneath her shapeless uniform.

SHE SMILES at her reflection in the window of the bus. She imagines him holding her, his strong arms wrapped around her. She closes her eyes and lets her mind run his fingers through her hair. He looks quite Asian. If he wasn't so stocky he might even pass for Indonesian. What would her mother say if she brought home a foreigner? She knows how impossible that would be.

EVERY NIGHT at the restaurant he sees young couples holding hands, and old couples ignoring one another. He lies on the bed thinking that if he could be with her he would never ignore her, even if she got old. They could grow old together. He could bring her back to Nepal. Her oriental features wouldn't look out of place. She could easily pass for a local. But she is a Muslim. He is a Hindu. How could that ever work? He's stupid even to think of it. And besides, it would be just like with his colleagues on the day shift, their jobs would never give them the free time to spend together. They are doomed to be separated by their work and by the clock.

He should put her out of his mind. What was he thinking? The best he can hope for is to save some money so that he can find a wife when he returns to Nepal. He has a sour taste in his mouth. It seems that in this country all his dreams are dashed. Back home everyone looked up to him. His mother was so proud that her son was going to fly in a plane and work overseas. But when he got here he was nobody. Just another restaurant worker not worth talking to. He is almost invisible. And lonely. Who would have thought that you could live in a place with so many people and be lonely? He knows that this is why his eyes have sought her out.

He wasn't at the car park this morning. She knows she shouldn't be disappointed, but she can't help herself. She shuffles onto the bus with all the other girls.

Each morning she still looks for him, but he is never there.

Girl with the Crooked Nose

"Think you can tipu me?" I shouted. "I don't want your smelly fish. I wouldn't feed it to a dog."

People stared. The fish auntie mumbled something. I felt bad about shouting at her. The other stall-holders gawked at me from behind piles of fresh ulam, jars of pickled fruit, displays of wide-eyed fish dreaming on beds of crushed ice.

"What are you looking at?" I picked up a tomato and threw it at an old man poking at a pile of slimy cuttlefish. He looked surprised and hurt.

"Pompuan gila. Get out of here, mad girl," shouted another stallholder, a heavyset man with a pockmarked face. I stuck out my tongue, embarrassed, yet thrilled by my own bad behaviour. I had never done anything like this before. I knew they would remember me and recognize me again.

I walked on past stalls of keropok, durian, crates of cockles, dismembered chickens, all too expensive for me, and exchanged coins for a few chillis. I couldn't come back from the market empty-handed.

Outside I raised a hand to shield my eyes from the blinding sunlight, then rummaged around in my handbag for my sunglasses. I turned the key in my kapchai and headed for home.

Dark clouds lurked over the water. Wind tugged at my hair and churned up froth on the waves.

I climbed the steps and kicked off my shoes on the wooden porch, leaving them beside two pairs of men's slippers. One pair was my father's, the other belonged to the man I had been told to call 'uncle'.

My father lay in his usual position on the mattress on the living room floor. His eyes were closed. I stood looking at him for a long moment. The man was in the bedroom, slouched across the mattress, his eyes gazing up at the rusty damp stains on the ceiling from where the roof leaked during monsoon, his trousers and underwear bundled around his ankles.

The clock was ticking. I dropped the plastic bag of chillis on the floor - my tiny spicy alibis - and held my phone, taking deep breaths, rehearsing what I would say. I tried to sound panicked. It wasn't difficult.

"Hello. Please help. Something happened. My father and his friend. Please come quickly." I gave my address, sobbingly answering questions.

I was sitting outside on the front porch when the police arrived. They took off their shoes and followed me indoors. I showed them the bodies. I manufactured tears.

"I just came home from the market," I explained. "I thought my father was asleep. He usually naps this time of day. Then I found his friend."

A policeman stretched a black and yellow plastic ribbon across the front of the house, one end tied to the mango tree, the other to the grey lamppost with the streetlight that never worked. An ambulance came. I didn't even have to fake my tears when they carried my father out on a stretcher with a GOOD MORNING towel draped over his face. A policewoman rubbed my back and consoled me. Then I was in the back of a police car that brought me to the balai polis.

A fluorescent light hummed and flickered.

"You need to change the starter," I said quietly.

"Apa?"

"The starter. For the light. If you change it the light will work better."

"Oh. Okay. So you say you do not know this other man?"

"I knew him, but not well. He was my father's friend, but any time he came to the house my father sent me out on an errand."

"Did you know about the drugs?"

"I saw ... I saw the syringe when I found the man in the bedroom. My father, he would not touch drugs. He was very sick."

The policewoman gave me a pitying look and wrote something on the paper fixed to her clipboard.

"What about family? You have someone you can stay with?"

I shook my head. "Not here. I have an aunt on the mainland, my mother's sister, but I can stay by myself."

"How old are you?"

"Fourteen."

TWO YEARS earlier my mother passed away, a week after my elder brother. Both died of dengue. Since then I lived alone with my father. I stopped school to look after him, to cook and do housework. I didn't mind. I didn't really like school anyway.

My father cried all the time. He hardly went to fish anymore. One night he came into my room and sat down on the mattress beside me.

"You know your father loves you," he said. "You mean so much to me. You're all I have left in the world." Then he drew me closer and showed me exactly how much he loved me. The next day he apologised, promising it wouldn't happen again. His promise lasted two weeks. I thought about running away, but I had nowhere to go.

Around this time my father started using, just once or twice a week to begin with, but soon every day. He stopped working on the fishing boats and granted himself a permanent residence visa for the mattress on the living room floor. We were running out of money. I earned a little by helping a neighbour make and sell popiah at the pasar malam, but it was just enough to buy rice and a few things to cook with the fish I caught from the river or the sea.

When I told the policewoman that my father sent me out of the house whenever the man appeared, I was telling the truth. I knew my father didn't like him. He had noticed the way the man licked his lips when he looked at me. But my father needed his fix. And there was no money.

"We can come to some arrangement," the man said to my father, looking across the room at me as I was getting ready to leave.

"No," said my father.

"Baiklah," said the man, standing up. "Call me when you have money."

He walked towards the door.

"Wait," my father called. He looked at me. I saw something change in his eyes. He looked back at the man and silently nodded. My father wouldn't look at me again.

The man smiled at my father. "You'll get your fix afterwards."

Then he grabbed me by the arm and dragged me into the bedroom.

"Stop," I said. "You're hurting me."

He slammed the door shut.

"So, are you going to help your father?"

"Leave me alone."

I tried to pull away but his grip was strong. Luckily he was holding me by my left arm. I punched him in the stomach as hard as I could. He released my arm and collapsed, winded, on the floor. I gave him a kick in the ribs for good measure and ran out of the room.

"You bastard," I screamed at my father, who was still on his mattress. "You bloody addict." I slapped him. I slapped him harder, again and again. He didn't try to defend himself, whimpering like a puppy being tortured.

I didn't hear the man come up behind me. He grabbed me by the throat and pulled me back into the bedroom, pushing me down onto the mattress. I couldn't breathe. With his free hand he ripped my clothes. He didn't let go of my neck until he had finished, then he punched me in the face. I heard my nose crack. Then he punched me again.

He was gone, leaving me with two black eyes, a bruised jaw, and a crooked nose. Over the following weeks the bruises went through all the colours of the rainbow, but my nose stayed the same crooked.

The man came back, of course, but not before allowing my father to experience a few days of withdrawal, sweating and writhing on his mattress. I hadn't forgiven my father, but he was still my father. I couldn't watch him suffer like this. He needed a fix. I tried to think of another way to get some heroin, but I had spent the last of our money on a big sack of rice. That was all we ate, along with whatever fish I could catch.

"Are you going to behave this time?" asked the man. I nodded. He followed me into the bedroom. This went on for months.

My bruises faded and I was able to work at the market again, but my father never recovered his health. He had grown so weak that he could hardly even feed himself. But even when I fed him he didn't want to eat. He only wanted one thing.

I learned how to heat the bent spoon with a cigarette lighter, how to work the syringe. My father insisted that I put the needle between his toes so there would be no tell-tale marks. I don't know who he thought he was fooling. His friends never called anymore and it had been a long time since he even left the house.

Every time the man came I took the heroin from him myself. I was the one paying for it after all. I told him I wanted a new clean syringe and needle, and I would be good to him if I could give my father his fix first. I didn't like the thought of my father lying there, listening to the both of us in the next room. With the drugs flowing in his veins he could drift away into whatever world he went to.

I reduced my father's dose, keeping back a little each time, and while I watched him get sicker I was building up a secret stash hidden in the kitchen. Two months later I had as much as I thought I needed. I prepared the syringe. I knew the man was due to arrive. I recognised the sound of his car engine, then his footsteps on the porch, the smell of Gudang Garam. I took the dadah from him and gave my father his dose while the man waited for his payment, smiling in anticipation. He was still rough, but if I didn't fight he wouldn't hit me. At least not in the face.

I put the needle between my father's toes, saw the blood rise up in the syringe and knew I had found a vein. I took a deep breath, then pushed the plunger home. My father opened his eyes wide and looked straight at me. Maybe I imagined it, but I thought I saw an expression of surprise, and then a look of gratefulness. With a low sigh, he closed his eyes.

"Let's get this over with," I said, turning to the man.

We had a familiar routine now. I had learned what he liked. He was sprawled on his back, hands behind his head, eyes closed, a big stupid smile on his face. While I worked him with one hand and my mouth I slowly reached the other hand under the edge of the mattress. My fingers found the hidden syringe. I pulled him out of my mouth and stabbed the needle deep into the mass of throbbing veins, quickly pushing the plunger down with my thumb. He jolted upright and stared in shock before falling back with a loud exhalation.

I wiped my fingerprints from the syringe with a tissue, then brought his hand down to take hold of it. I left the room, quickly checking on my father before going to the market. His face was grey, his skin almost cold. Otherwise he looked as if he was just asleep.

THE POLICE never checked my alibi. Weeks later, I went back to the market. I asked the fish auntie if she remembered me. She did. I apologised for shouting at her.

"Takpa sayang. We all have bad days," she said with motherly kindness.

I just nodded and smiled.

Bed of Roses

You should be ashamed of yourself, lying there on that dirty greasy thing. It smells of piss. You smell of piss. You have to get a hold of yourself. When was the last time you changed your cardboard? You should get a new one at least once a week. Have some self-respect. Look at me. My nails are cut, my clothes are clean. I change my cardboard every night. While you sleep on that damp filthy thing, I lie on a bed of roses, lilies, lotus flowers. You don't believe me? I'll show you the florist shop. I'm there every day. I know when the deliveries are made. All I have to do is ask them for a box for you as well. They'll give it, no problem. They always do. You can breathe in the smell of flowers instead of that plastic bag of glue.

Kurang Manis

There was a blister on his thumb where he had burned it that morning. He had surprised his mother with an unannounced visit, parking his kapchai outside the house in the shade of the old mango tree. Mynahs chattered in the branches, gossiping to pass the time while they waited for the small hard green fruit to swell and ripen. The door was unlocked, as usual. No matter how many times he told his mother it wasn't safe she just shrugged and pointed out that there was nothing in the house worth stealing.

His father's photograph stared down sternly from his frame on the wall, bedecked with a garland of jasmine flowers today and a grey smudge of vibuthi applied to his forehead. That generation never smiled in photos, preferring to honour the formal occasion of being photographed with a measure of dignity, wary that smiling might be interpreted as being frivolous, unserious. After so many years he could no longer picture his father's face in real life. Had he ever smiled? Surely he must have. Instead his memories of his father were mostly of the stale tobacco smell of the cigarettes he smoked all day, the ones that ruined his lungs and left his mother a young widow and left him half an orphan, and the smell of Old Spice aftershave when he dressed up in a starched vesthi for special occasions, though what those occasions might have been, he couldn't remember now. Respecting traditions, his mother never remarried. Once was more than enough to make that mistake in any case, she often said. Anyway, any potential suitors might have been put off by the black and white photo surveying the hallway, vetting every person as they entered the home and again as they left. Perhaps that was why she had placed the portrait so prominently, a warning to others, a reminder to herself.

His mother was in the kitchen. His approach was masked by the loud hiss of the pressure cooker, the valve spinning percussively at high speed. He tapped her on the left shoulder, and then as she turned he ducked to the right and reached around to flip the chapati on the tawa. It was meant to be a joke, but he got burned for his trouble, though it hadn't really hurt at the time.

"Run it under some water, you stupid boy," his mother scolded, turning off the gas fire under the pressure cooker. "Why you always want to interfere in kitchen business? You can't see that I am busy?"

He laughed in reply and saw his mother's lips tighten as she tried to suppress a smile.

"Here, hold this on it," she said, handing him an ice cube from the freezer compartment of the ancient refrigerator. The paintwork was scabbed in several places, rings of rust bursting through the white surface like some skin disease. The machine rattled and hummed and groaned throughout the day and night, almost as much a presence and part of the family as a pet. He had promised her many times that when he had enough money he would buy her a new one to replace it, but like a pet, or even like his father, he knew his mother would only part with the refrigerator once it was dead.

"No need Amma. It doesn't hurt."

"Try. I read on my Wazzarp group that ice is best for blisters. I want to see if it is true."

Instead he grinned and popped the ice cube in his mouth, crunching it loudly between his teeth.

"Stupid boy," his mother said again, quieter this time, shaking her head.

HE WAITED for the traffic lights to change. The blister had swollen into a tight bubble that stretched the skin, begging to be punctured to let the water out. He could almost hear his mother telling him to leave it alone. Stupid boy. He had stayed for lunch. She had insisted that if he wasn't going to participate in her ice cube experiment he should rub the blister with coconut oil, from the blue Parachute brand plastic bottle. After they had eaten she applied a hastily made paste of turmeric and rosewater on his burn. Now he would spend the next week with the inconvenience of a yellow thumb that would indelibly stain everything he touched. Mothers. How did she flip chapatis with her bare hands without ever getting burned? Or did she get blisters just like his when she was still a girl learning to cook from her own mother? She probably just had heatproof hands, just one of the supernatural powers he might have ascribed to her when he was a boy, like her laser vision that could see through walls, or her sense of smell that could tell if he had been smoking or drinking with Faizal and Ishak and the other boys when they all should have been at school studying for the SPM.

The lights finally turned green and he jostled briefly with the other motorcyclists before traffic began to flow again. Beneath the helmet sweat soaked his scalp, running down his neck, his forehead, cooled by the breeze of movement. He glanced at his watch. He would get there on time, maybe even early. It was good to be early. It showed eagerness, enthusiasm, respect.

HE SAT down on one of the plastic chairs, facing out to the street so that he could see the man arrive. Another five minutes. He ordered a teh tarik kurang manis, then kicked off his slippers and drew his feet up onto the seat to sit more comfortably cross-legged. A lazy ceiling fan unenthusiastically stirred the heavy air. The waiter plonked the tea down in front of him, a small wave washing over the side of the glass, forming a murky puddle on the table. He wanted to ask the boy to wipe the table, but the waiter had already turned, either not having noticed or not caring about the spilt tea. He couldn't catch the attention of any of the other staff, so he stood up, slipping the thongs of his slippers between his toes, and grabbed a handful of pink paper napkins from the pile on the counter, accidentally pressing on the blister as he did so. It hurt. He had never thought about how often he used this part of his thumb, but now its sensitivity made it impossible to ignore. Scrolling through the feeds on the screen of his phone, gripping the handle on the tea glass, eating earlier, it seemed everything he touched used that same part of his thumb. If he held a pen or wore shoes with laces he would probably put pressure on the blister too. Sometimes you take things for granted, not giving them a second thought until they become too painful to bear. He should have used the ice cube instead of eating it, a lesson learned the hard way, the only way he ever seemed to learn. Maybe he should have listened to his mother's Wazzarp aunties' advice and acted while there was still time. He could ask the waiter for an ice cube, though it was probably too late now. The damage was done and healing would be a slow process. Besides, the workers seemed deeply involved in a discussion they were having in a language he couldn't understand. Nepali? Bengali? Burmese? It was hard to tell where anyone was from these days, so many foreigners. Just a few years ago, when he was still at school, the mamak stall staff almost always spoke Tamil or Malay, or both. Sometimes it didn't even feel like he was in his own country anymore. Maybe this is what it felt like for those who couldn't accept sharing a country with others after so many generations. Not all of them of course. Not his old drinking buddies from school who tried to break every rule and convention just on principle. They saw each other as people first, no matter what food they ate at home or what language they spoke with their grandparents. But the politicians, the ones in power anyway, kept going on about how they were this first, and that only second. Or maybe even third, because they had to bring religion into it too. He accompanied his mother to the temple for the festivals, even knew some of the prayers, or enough of them that he could mumble along and make it look like he did, but religion didn't play a big part in his life. Why should it? If everyone would just mind their own business then the world would be a better place.

The staff had finished their discussion and were now busily wiping tables, taking orders from the throng of late afternoon customers, cooking roti canai and thosai on the big rectangular hot plate. Did they ever burn their thumbs when they cooked? Had their mothers taught them to use ice cubes to cool and stop the damage before it was too late, or was that just a modern Wazzarp auntie thing, as useless in real life as the rest of the fake news they so willingly spread?

THE MAN he had come to meet finally arrived, half an hour late, not that he would dare say anything about being kept waiting. He was big, with big hair, thick and black, worn longer at the back than on the top and sides. He had dark sunglasses propped atop his head and the kind of upper lip that looked like it should have been sporting a bushy moustache but was clean-shaven instead, like the rest of the man's face. His large fingers were decorated in half a dozen rings, which in turn were decorated with the kind of semi-precious stones that promise virility and good health and financial success — probably, especially for the one selling the ring — but his fingernails were bitten short with jagged edges. They talked, then the man talked, explaining the job, what it would entail, what would be expected of him. He nodded as the man spoke, thinking how the money would make it worthwhile despite the risks involved. He would surprise his mother with a new refrigerator for real this time, get it delivered directly from the shop so that she couldn't refuse.

It all happened so fast. They weren't wearing uniforms, so he didn't understand who they were at first. All he knew was that he was shielding his head with his arms as they beat him with their sticks. Then he was handcuffed and pushed into the back of a car. He saw the big man being dragged towards another car and watched as he fought back, lashing out with his feet. He managed to catch one of the policeman square between the legs, sending him to his knees with his hands clutching his groin. Then the man ran towards another car that had pulled up with its passenger door open, jumped inside and sped away. He never saw the man again, and when the policemen asked he told them that he had never met the man before either. But they wouldn't listen.

It was cold, but the pathologist enjoyed the temperature. Compared to the sultry heat outdoors the air felt clean and crisp, like a room-sized refrigerator. It was one of the perks of the job. Maybe the only perk. He looked at the body, its shape still hidden beneath the sheet, yet another one brought here directly from the lokap under cover of darkness.

"Kidney failure," said the uniformed policeman.

The pathologist looked at the policeman, a young man, but obviously already initiated, then lowered his gaze.

"You know how it works," said the policeman with a sigh. "Just write what the boss says to write. Kidney failure." The policeman took one last look at the body, shook his head, then turned and left.

Alone with the body now, the pathologist slowly lifted the sheet. He looked at the grey face, the swollen eyes, puffed up and discoloured, the nose crooked, clearly broken. Clumps of hair had been torn out, taking pieces of scalp with them. The lips were swollen too. He already knew that when he opened the mouth he would find smashed teeth. Victim, a young man, late teens, possibly early twenties. Multiple contusions. Fractured maxillary. Possible mandibular fracture ...

He paused when examining the ears. At first he thought it was some kind of earring, it was hard to keep up with fashions these days, but no, this was something else. He took a magnifying glass, then tweezers and eased the thin sliver of metal out of the cold cartilage. A staple, the same kind he would use to clasp the pages of his autopsy report together. Though he had seen the results of all kinds of depravity during his long career, this was new. There wasn't just one staple either. Both ears had been perforated and fastened to the young man's scalp with at least a dozen more staples. He used a pencil to part the hair and found more staples embedded in the scalp. He tried to prise one out with the tweezers but it was firmly fixed into the cranium, embedded into the parietal bone. He wondered with a shudder how much force that might have required.

The body, as expected, bore multiple acute lesions, burns, and bruises. A dislocated shoulder. At least three ribs were broken, the imprint of a boot heel clearly visible on the skin, the most probable proximate cause of death, not immediately, but later, slowly, from punctured organs and internal bleeding, though the victim might already have been unconscious by then. No visible lacerations or any signs of exsanguination. The hands were ruined, the distorted fingers swollen at the joints, pointing off in unnatural directions, the all too familiar ring-shaped impact wounds from where they had been broken with a hammer. Missing fingernails, of course. That was probably where they had started. On the thumb of the right hand there was a burst blister, cause uncertain, but certainly unrelated to the other wounds, since it was the bright yellow of iodine, the only one of the injuries that had been treated. He lowered his head and sniffed the young man's thumb. No, not iodine. It was turmeric, a common enough folk remedy for burns and a reasonably effective antiseptic.

The pathologist pulled the sheet back over the body and sat down. He pinched the ridge of his nose, then leaned forward with his elbows on his knees, the mounds of his hands pushed into his eye sockets, triggering the pulse-slowing oculocardiac reflex, as if that could remove the things he was forced to see. He sat there for a long time in the cold brightly lit silence. He had a choice between using scalpels and saws to further disfigure the body for a full autopsy and writing up an honest report, though that should really be the job of a forensic pathologist, or he could just slide the broken battered body back into its drawer and go upstairs to type and sign and stamp the certificate that said, cause of death: kidney failure. Either way, his choice would have consequences, for the victim's family, for himself, the potential price he would have to pay all too evident, embodied in the cold still shape under the sheet. He already knew which path he would take. He was no hero. Nothing he could do would bring this young man back to life. He had once taken a Hippocratic Oath to protect life. Through his silence and compliance the lives he would be protecting would be his family's and his own. Plus there would be the usual envelope that accompanied these cases. He could take the family out for dinner, maybe even a short holiday away from the island, a long weekend in a resort in the cool hills on the mainland. It would be good to get away, to put some distance between himself and here.

THE KAPCHAI STOOD on the roadside near the mamak stall for almost two weeks before someone stole the headlight. After that it went fast. The brake cables were taken, the petrol tank siphoned, then the wheels, the exhaust muffler, the tail light and turn signals, the chain, the shock absorbers, even the footpads. Soon all that was left was the bare skeleton with the seat. Then one night someone set fire to the seat and a black sticky melted mess dripped onto the ground. After that the charred and rusted carcass was taken away, maybe by officials from the bandaraya, maybe by scrap metal merchants. The puddle of molten plastic hardened on the ground, where it remains to this day, slowly weathered by the heat of the sun and monsoon rains, an indelible stain, an unrecognised memorial to a young man who wanted to surprise his mother with a new refrigerator, a young man who once burned his thumb while flipping a chapati.

Big Balls

Aziz always teases me about my balls. Always the same jokes about spending all my time playing with my balls, or having the biggest set of balls of anyone he knows. I've heard his lines so often they're not funny anymore, but he thinks he's hilarious. I picture the row of pins as his teeth and send the ball rumbling down the wooden lane to smash them, sending them flying everywhere. One day I'll do it for real and use my fist instead. He won't laugh so much then. But for the moment I just grin and fake a laugh. I have to. I make sure he's always there at the competitions. I get him tickets, and any time he wants to go bowling I make sure he doesn't pay. I even share my cigarettes with him. I need to keep him happy. If he ever tells about what happened with his little sister it will mean a lot of trouble.

It was her own fault. If she hadn't insisted on coming along to the competition in Ipoh it never would have happened.

"Oh Firdaus, please let me come," she whined. What was I supposed to do?

She was asking for it anyway. That sort of girl is always asking for it. I knew how old she was but with her make-up and her jeans she looked much older, at least sixteen. And the shape of her little body in that tight t-shirt – no man could resist. Waving her hands in the air like that when she cheered, showing off her little tits. Not even wearing a tudung. You know the kind of girl I mean. No modesty.

In the hotel room later on she kept on laughing. Aziz knew that she was with me. He must have known what would happen. Dirty little slut. She got nervous when I touched her, but I know that's what she wanted all along, even if she pretended that she didn't. I had to slap her when she tried to push my hands away. I didn't slap her hard, and only once or twice, but she started crying and kept sobbing as I pulled off her jeans. It would have been much easier if she wore a skirt, but then it wouldn't have shown off the outline of her tight little ass. I put my hand over her mouth to shut her up.

Afterwards she said she would report me to the police. I said if she told anyone I would kill her and throw her body in a canal, stripped naked for everyone to see, so that everyone would know what kind of whore she was. The police never came, so I suppose she never told. It wasn't any good anyhow. She got me so excited that it was all over in a minute. I can't really blame her for that. The blood on the sheets was enough to let me know that she had no experience. If she had calmed down I would have done it to her a second time, a third time, but with all that blood and tears she disgusted me. I told her to get dressed and go back to her room with her brother.

I was surprised she was still a virgin. Aziz always seemed like the kind of guy who would do it with his sister and then boast about it later, like the ones at school. Some of them even recorded it on their phones and showed it in the playground. Mostly it was just with her mouth, but sometimes it was from behind, in either hole. It made me sort of sick to see their cocks, but I got hard all the same and had to go take care of it in the school toilets imagining that if I had a sister how I would do it to her too.

Aziz must know. He must have guessed, but he never mentioned it. He probably thinks it's not a big deal. He's right. Why these girls get so upset I don't know. It's only natural. What do they think that they are for? A woman should serve a man and satisfy his desires. I like those women from the Obedient Wives Club. They understand what's right.

Anyway that all happened a long time ago. Now she's fifteen and pregnant, which just goes to show that she's a slut. The kid is not mine, I only did it to her that once.

She doesn't come to the bowling competitions anymore and she stopped wearing those revealing clothes. Now she dresses properly, covering her hair and everything except her hands and face. She should cover that as well – she always looks so miserable, not like before when she laughed and smiled. I sometimes wonder if that's because of what happened in the hotel, but you can never understand women anyway. Probably she's trying to be a serious girl to make up for her sins, or maybe she's thinking about her baby. Some say fifteen is too young to have a baby, but that doesn't make any sense. If she's old enough to get pregnant she's old enough.

I didn't think of her getting pregnant that time in the hotel. I was too horny to worry about things like that. If she did, she must have got rid of it. All the girls know where to go for that, finding some bomoh who will give them herbs to drink that will make them sick. But maybe she didn't get pregnant and there's something wrong with me. What if I can't make a woman pregnant? What sort of man would that make me? I would be a laughing stock. They would call me pondan and say I am not a real man.

I suppose I will find out when I get married. My parents are still looking for the right girl for me. I would like to choose for myself, but they say I shouldn't worry about such things, I am still young and have a bright future. Everyone says I have a bright future, so it must be true. I should just focus on my bowling, they advise. Practice, practice, practice. So I spend every day in the air-conditioned alley playing with my balls, the biggest balls around, scoring strikes and watching the pinsetter gather up the pins so I can play again, dreaming of the day when I will represent my country and be a hero to my people.

Banu

Banu watched the logging camp from the forest's edge. In the shadows of the giant trees she was almost invisible. Cicadas screeched their whining song. The men were washing and cooking after their day's work, the air filled with the woodsmoke that rose from a small cooking fire. Most of the men were shirtless. Thin but muscular. Visibly tired. Banu could hear their voices but could not make out their words. A langur they had shot was skewered on a stick and roasting over the embers. To Banu the peeled unmoving body looked just like a human baby and made her hate the men even more. But she took some consolation that they would be plagued that night by the monkey's fleas. Eat and be eaten. Banu knew all about fleas, how their bites were more painful and itched for longer than mosquito bites.

This wasn't the first time she had come here to watch the loggers. When they were away during the day she walked through their shelter and rifled through their things, but beyond the thin sweat-stained foam mattresses and a few clothes and bars of soap they didn't seem to own much. She should have been at school, but being here was better than enduring the beatings the teacher gave her and her classmates. Sometimes he made them hold their ears and squat as punishment for unknown transgressions. Other days he made them stand out in the hot sun without anything to drink, showing that he had power over them, that he could do whatever he wanted and get away with it. The day he slid his greasy hand inside Banu's t-shirt she decided that she would no longer go to school, not even if her mother scolded her. She learned nothing from this teacher. Though that wasn't entirely true. She learned than men can be as cruel and dangerous as any of the spirits who lived in the forest.

But it wasn't that Banu didn't want to learn. The arrival of the loggers opened a door to another world she could only dimly imagine. She observed while staying hidden, the loggers never knowing or suspecting that they were being spied upon by a curious eleven-year-old girl.

They had appeared a few months earlier. First they made a track, cutting a wide line through the forest. She remembered the sight of the smouldering stumps, how the smoke had filled the air for days. Even when she went back to the settlement where her family lived the smell stayed in her nostrils, while the whine of the chainsaws still rang in her ears. Then the loggers brought big groaning machines to dig up what was left of the charred stumps, huge tangles of blackened broken roots that were pushed to one side, leaving the bare earth exposed, a pinkish clay that looked like a wound.

When the rains came the water gathered in murky puddles that mirrored the empty sky when the rainfall stopped, reflecting clouds where once were treetops. The clay that had lain hidden beneath the forest floor now turned to sticky mud and the water in the stream that ran through the exposed patch of ground no longer ran clear downstream.

Despite having everything they needed to build a shelter at hand, the loggers used heavy big-wheeled trucks to bring the flat sheets of wood and ribbed sheets of corrugated iron that they nailed to a frame made of pre-cut beams of timber. Her father and uncles had laughed. Were these loggers too simple to understand that a roof of nipah palm would have been quicker and much easier to build? That it would protect them from the heat of the sun, instead of amplifying it. These newcomers clearly knew nothing about living in the forest, but everything about destroying it.

Banu watched the men until the light started to fade, the screech of the cicadas slowing with the cooling air. She tried to understand how the loggers could spend their days ravaging all the beauty around them. Most of the birds had fled the area, frightened away by the noise of the machines. When they returned to their roosts at night they circled in confusion, the once familiar trees strangely missing.

As the trees began to fall the animals had run away too, which pleased her father and uncles for a while. Straying into unfamiliar territory, the disorientated boar and deer were easier to track and hunt, and Banu and her extended family had eaten and shared more meat than usual, at first. But the animals that escaped the blowpipe darts soon learned the unfamiliar terrain and became more wary prey, and the family's hunting grounds were disappearing every day the loggers worked.

Banu watched the men sharing the monkey they had cooked, tearing the limbs from the tiny body. Then she turned from the raw wound of the logger's encampment and made her way through the familiar forest, her feet moving silently as she made her way between the giant columns of trees, wondering whether they would be spared and survive the onslaught of the loggers' noisy chainsaws.

THIRTY YEARS HAD CHANGED the town, but Pastor John still recognised it as the place where he had once grown up. Beneath the plastic banners and hoardings the old shop facades were still the same, even if many of the original retailers had long gone out of business. Now the five-foot-way was flanked with vape shops and places selling cheap and colourful phone cases. A few of the old businesses were boarded up, but Mister Tan's hardware shop was till there, as was Mister Tan himself. The two men expressed surprise at seeing one another after such a long interval and chatted with an easy familiarity they had never shared as younger men.

"Just back for visit?" asked Mister Tan.

"No, we decided to come back home to retire. My pension can stretch a lot further here and besides, there's no place like home."

"Where were you? Australia? Canada? Some place like that?"

"The UK. But it has changed so much. It's no longer the place we moved to. So expensive these days. And it's getting harder to be a foreigner."

"Brexit?"

"Yes, the usual story. You people coming here to steal our jobs they say, as if anyone could steal a job. If they want to be angry about foreigners working in their country they should blame their fellow countrymen for giving foreigners jobs. Nasty. Brexit made things worse for us. It didn't feel safe there anymore. It was time to go. Time to come back home. And how about you?"

"Still here. But everything else is also changing. People only want to shop in the air-con mall outside the town now. Business here is no good anymore."

"And your children?"

"All overseas. Melbourne. Toronto. Even got one daughter in Dusseldorf, the youngest girl. I tell them go make life somewhere else. Nothing here. I think this also maybe my last year. See which daughter will let us live with them. Spend time with our grandchildren. Grandfather started this shop before the Japanese war. Busy then. Now some days not even one customer, or only Bangladeshi workers from the plantations. But what can they buy? A new pair of rubber boots? A fishing net? A rat trap? A parang? Best business now is spare parts for chainsaws. Without that I close already."

"Chainsaws?"

"Loggers. You travel up the hills you will for sure no longer recognise. All the forest gone already. Even the rubber plantations finish. Palm oil, palm oil, palm oil. Plantation after plantation. They say it is good business, but only for a special few. Not to anyone in town anyway. Nearly everyone gone now, retired or overseas. Like I say, things have changed."

"But I thought the town was doing well in general? That huge new road is very nice, with all that grass and those palm trees. The shopping mall. Very modern. And the new golf course is already very famous. Designed by Rimau Kayu, or one of those celebrity golf chaps isn't it? There was even an article about it in the in-flight magazine."

"You know who all owns that golf course? You know who owns all the logging companies?"

"No, who?"

"Members of the royal family."

"I thought the plantations were private businesses."

"Another kind of royalty. But they all help each other. Politicians too. All like a club. Get up on a stage and say 'you help me, I help you.' Don't even have the shame to hide their corruption and their wealth. Here I will take the timber, make lots of money, then I sell the land, make even more money, then negotiate a percentage on palm oil profits, more money. Like that also can. Buy big boats and build new palaces. These flers got so much money they don't know what to do with it. That big road, they use to race their Ferraris and Porsches and don't know what all else."

"You sound angry."

"Of course I'm angry. They steal my children's future. Even scoring Seven A in SPM they still cannot go into their universities. We are always second-class citizens here, and always will be. Maybe you away too long you forget already. And then their own people. How many of them in poverty? Marrying their children to old men for money for rice. What kind of life is that?"

"I know it's still a work in progress, but there have been many improvements. There's electricity. Better WiFi than the UK."

"These flers use this internet for their propaganda. That's the only reason it is so important for them. Cybertroopers spreading lies. But someone tell the truth cannot. Can go direct to lokap only. What to say? I think you make a mistake to come back here. Holiday can. Very nice. Proper food. But fulltime lah? What to say? I only hope you don't regret."

Pastor John left the hardware shop feeling disheartened, not so much about material things Mister Tan had talked about, though he hadn't quite seen things from that perspective before, and wasn't entirely sure if everything the shopkeeper was entirely objective or factual. No, what troubled Pastor John more was the fact that he had left the old man clearly more agitated and upset than he had been before he had decided to call in and say hello. As a pastor surely his role was to make a positive difference in people's lives, but by allowing their conversation to take such an unexpected turn he had clearly failed in this instance.

Instead of leaving the hardware shop empty-handed, he had bought a pair of rubber boots, not really needing them but not knowing what else to buy, feeling a duty towards the shopkeeper, ceding to the suggestion made about the Bangladeshi workers' shopping habits, while reassuring himself that a good pair of rubber boots always came in handy. And even if they didn't he could always give them away to someone who might have more use for them.

"BUT I WAS BORN HERE on the island," said Pastor John, trying not to let his frustration show. "I grew up here."

He had sat for more than three hours in the crowded hall waiting to hear his number called so that he could speak to the immigration officer through the tiny gap at the bottom of the glass window.

"I understand sir, but you cannot have it both ways. When you were here you wanted to leave, but after you left you wanted to come back. When you left the island you gave up your citizenship. You made that decision not us. All we are doing is respecting your decision. The maximum period you can stay here is one year. After that you can apply again."

"So if I apply again in one year I can continue living here?"

"We cannot guarantee. Come back in one year and apply again. Only then you will get the answer."

Pastor John rubbed his face with his hands.

"Alright. So in one year's time what documents will I need?"

"We cannot say, sir. It changes all the time. But each application will be treated as the first."

"This is very frustrating. Very disappointing."

"I understand sir, but please understand that we are only doing our jobs here. We do not make the rules, we just apply them."

"I understand. And there's really no other solution possible?"

"No other official solution, no."

"Meaning there might be an unofficial solution?"

"You say you were born and raised here. You know how things work."

"I see. I think I understand what you are saying. If I wanted to have a coffee or something is there a place nearby you would recommend?"

"Personally, I like the Ocean Sun restaurant. Do you know it? It is quiet and discreet and they do good seafood, fresh from the sea."

"I don't know it, but I can find it. What time would be the best time to eat there?"

"Seven o'clock is usually a good time. You can enjoy the sunset."

PASTOR JOHN TRIED to remember the immigration officer's face and wondered if he would recognise the man out of uniform. But that didn't matter. The immigration officer found him and sat down beside him, facing out towards the advertised ocean view and a suitably stunning sunset. They ordered food, Pastor John's treat of course, then when they finished eating the man named a figure. Pastor John countered with a much lower number. Eventually they agreed on a price lower than the initial figure, but still what must have been equivalent to at least one month of the immigration officer's salary. In return, within the week Pastor John had a stamp in his passport that would allow him to live and work on the island for a period of five years. He would have preferred something more permanent, but five years gave him room to breathe.

DESPITE BEING from the mainland Preacher Kazir had a huge following on the island. He had a weekly television show, a podcast, with new episodes whenever he found the time to record and upload them. But most importantly he had his own brand of permitted foods and cosmetics, so that his followers could be sure not to pollute their bodies while purifying their minds. Running the company took up more time than preaching, but both were two sides of the same coin. A cynical observer might have pointed out that his sermons were little more than glorified advertisements for his food and cosmetics business, but invariably that cynical observer would then be hounded on social media by the preacher's devotees, some of them going as far as issuing death threats to anyone who dared call into question the integrity of the preacher's brand. With that sort of customer fidelity, Kazir was well on his way to buying a second yacht and seriously considering a new range of clothing that would be both reassuringly expensive while covering and hiding any hint of the real shape of his female devotees' bodies. He made a note to ask one of his P.A.s if there was anyone in the devotee database who was a fashion designer or who might happen to own a sweatshop where the garments could be cheaply made.

But all these were worldly concerns. He had to work hard to maintain his focus on the important business of saving souls. To this end he was working with a firm of architects to design an easy-to-assemble prayer hall that could be mass-produced and flat-packed and shipped on trucks, ready to be assembled and placed all over the island, and perhaps, if it was successful, even on the mainland. Each prayer hall would have a small shop attached, where all the products from his brand could be sold as well, because it would be stupid to miss out on the opportunity to make more sales and revenue.

But he insisted that the architects make the shops discreet, that they shouldn't distract devotees from his sermons, though now that he thought of it, if he followed through with this clothing idea, and why shouldn't he, the shops might need to be slightly larger than they were on the latest draft blueprints.

As for the sermons, they would be beamed live by satellite internet connections into every prayer hall, so that all his devotees could hear the same thing at the same time, giving them the reassurance that they would always benefit from the same standardised level of excellence regardless of where on the island they happened to be attending. At least that was the plan.

It was ambitious, certainly, and wouldn't necessarily be simple to achieve, but the preacher didn't get to where he was without dreaming big or knowing whose palms needed to be greased for things to happen on the island.

PASTOR JOHN'S four-wheel drive car was parked in the clearing beside the logger's hut. Apart from two clear intersecting arcs on the windshield, the car was covered in mud, though Banu knew that the colour of the hidden paintwork was originally grey. She also knew Pastor John, everyone did, but he had never driven here before. In the past he parked much further downhill, on the tarred roadside beside the near-invisible trailhead, close to the simple hut where her mother sometimes sold bottled honey and bundles of petai to visitors from the towns and cities on the mainland. He would make the long walk to the settlement where he would be shyly welcomed. Then he would sit and rest while various family members followed the trail back to his car, curious to see what Pastor John might have brought this time.

Sometimes there were bundles of old clothes with words written on them in English. Sweets for the children, though they were shared among everyone, or cooking utensils, though Banu preferred the flavour of food cooked in lengths of bamboo. Always there were heavy bags of rice, salt and sugar, and more often than not, cans of condensed milk. They didn't need the food, the forest provided all they needed, but it was easier than digging out tubers and the sweetened milk made a change.

Pastor John usually stayed a day or two, talking with the elders, checking on the health of the children and any new babies. He was a thin old man with wrinkled skin. When Banu was very young Pastor John used to come to with a woman who might have been his wife. Or maybe they were just friends. But whoever the old woman was she was no longer able or willing to make the steep climb to the settlement. Maybe she had died. Banu wondered about these things, but not enough that she would ever voice her questions out loud.

Before they ate Pastor John said a few prayers to his god and the adults nodded seriously, waiting patiently for him to finish. Banu's people had their own beliefs, but Pastor John was just one of many who wanted to believe in something else. Instead of speaking to the spirits of the forest Pastor John spoke to a god who lived in the sky, far above the clouds in a place where Pastor John promised they would all go to when they died, if they agreed to believe in his God. Being eleven years old Banu had long understood that when things died they didn't go to the sky, they went into the ground, feeding the forest as it had fed them, but Pastor John was a kind man and one of the few people who ever came to visit.

Preacher Kazir looked up from his spreadsheet, allowing a satisfied smile to linger on his lips. This year's figures were good. In fact they had exceeded his targets, and by no small amount. When trying to understand why his projections had been so much lower than the actual results it soon became clear that it was simply because he had underestimated the number of new converts and the exponential growth they brought, mostly thanks to the heavy discounts given for any devotees who could bring two or more new souls into the fold. In turn these new converts, eager to gain access to the preacher's branded products at bargain prices, each brought in new converts, who in turn further spread his reach.

So far five prototype prayer halls had been successfully assembled, all of them equipped with fibre-optic broadband connections. The locations had been chosen on that basis, his technical manager arguing that wireless satellite connections would really only be necessary and more suited to the remotest of locations.

As it happened, one such remote location had recently become a little more accessible, thanks to a new logging road that cut deep into some of the remotest parts of the island's forests. Better yet there were people living there, simple people who knew little of the outside world or of God's plans for them. It would be the perfect location to test run a completely off-grid prayer hall, one with solar panels on the roof and perhaps a little wind turbine generator if there happened to be a crosswind.

There was just one snag. Kazir's sources had informed him that a pastor from a different franchise had been observed paying regular visits to the people there. But the righteous path is beset with obstacles, and it wouldn't be the first time the preacher faced competition. He believed fervently in the strength of his brand, bolstered by the enthusiasm of his increasingly engaged devotees. Their fervour could be harnessed to his advantage. No, there was no way a meddling soul-stealing pastor was going to stand in the way of Preacher Kazir's dreams of total market domination.

BANU ACCOMPANIED Pastor John back to his car, along with several other people from the settlement. They waved goodbye, not knowing when they would see him again, though the old man had promised to return with more supplies before the next rains, including textbooks and pens and paper, and hopefully, with luck, a young dynamic teacher who would revive the abandoned school.

He already had the perfect candidate in mind, a young woman from a good family who regularly attended prayer meetings in the town. Her fiancé had recently jilted her and left for overseas, like so many of the young people, or anyone who could afford to. While prayer and the support of the small community helped, it was through the path of action that she would find herself again. Yes, running the school would be the perfect project to give meaning to the young woman's life and help her mend her broken heart.

Banu cut across the hairpin bends, moving swiftly downhill through the ugly clearings that had so recently been part of this great forest that once covered the entire island. Each time she caught sight of Pastor John's car she waved, smiling, and saw the old man smile in return, though his hands were clutching the steering wheel too tightly on the bumpy track for him to risk a wave in return.

From the clearing Banu plunged into the stretch of forest that still grew along the tarred road. The loggers had spared a stretch wide enough that any passing motorists would never even begin to suspect the devastated landscape that lay began just a few hundred metres from the roadside, vast clearings that exposed hills and valleys and bare earth where once had been a sea of trees. Though the huge tree trunks chained to the beds of trucks that regularly made their way down the tarred road might have alerted anyone even half-observant to the extent of the deforestation.

Banu squatted in the trees by the roadside, hidden in the shadows, ready to spring out and wave goodbye to Pastor John one last time, the smell of sun-baked tar hot in her nostrils. But she didn't move from her hiding place.

Instead she watched as two big black cars with tinted windows blocked the road in front of Pastor John's car, while another two cars pulled up behind him. Doors were opened and men dressed in black quickly emerged, holding what could only have been guns, though they were very different guns to the one her grandfather kept wrapped in an oily cloth.

They wore black masks that covered their faces, and goggles that covered their eyes, so that they all looked the same, all moving quickly as if controlled by one mind. Pastor John was roughly pulled from his car and bundled into the back of one of the black cars, while one of the men took Pastor John's place behind his steering wheel. Then they were gone, leaving just the smell of their exhaust fumes.

The whole operation had taken less than a minute, happening so fast that Banu wondered if she had imagined the whole scene. She was trembling now and noticed that she was squatting over a patch of ground soaked with her own pee. Her mother had once told her of being this afraid the time she had come face to face with a tiger in the forest while picking fern heads when she was just a girl only Banu's age.

Banu would have to tell her family what she had seen. They would believe her because they knew that she only told the truth. She was not a storyteller, she didn't have that skill, and even if she did what she had witnessed was far beyond anything her imagination was capable of conjuring up. She would have to tell what had happened to Pastor John, but what was there to tell? Who were these men who had taken him? There was so much about the world beyond the forest that Banu still did not understand, perhaps would never understand.

THE CLOUDS BLOCKED the stars on a moonless night as the men rolled the blue plastic barrel down the loose planks that connected the boat to the jetty's edge. It was a straightforward job, but it wouldn't do for the barrel to fall into the water, at least not yet. The barrel was heavy, half-filled with the concrete they had poured over the old man's folded body. He had hardly weighed a thing and was easy to fit into the barrel, not like some of the others the men had dealt with before, who needed to be cut into pieces first.

The barrel safely aboard, the planks were withdrawn. Three men stayed in the boat while the others returned to the black vehicles. The little boat's outboard motor chugged to life, a quieter engine than the noisy long-tailed boats the local fishermen liked to use. The man at the stern let the motor run at a low speed. There was no hurry, no lights visible on this quiet side of the island, though in the distance on the horizon the lights of towns and villages twinkled from the mainland, so near, yet a world away. It was a still night, with no wind and the boat drew a small wake behind it in the water, the liquid path soon erased.

They left the coast of the island far behind, until they were close to midway to the mainland, a place where the men knew that the water was deepest, a place where a weighted barrel could rest undisturbed and undiscovered, as if it had never even existed. Over time shellfish and seaweeds would make their homes on the smooth blue plastic, slowly colonising it until it was covered, absorbed and camouflaged, just another part of the sea bed.

The helmsman cut the motor and allowed the boat to drift to a silent stop. When they heaved the barrel overboard the boat rocked violently. One of the men laughed nervously as he staggered to keep his balance, but the barrel had hardly made a splash and sank instantly beneath the inky dark surface of the sea.

Then the outboard chugged again, the propellers gurgling and spluttering as they were lowered into the water. None of the men spoke on the return journey, though the helmsman lit a cigarette, the red tip glowing intermittently in the darkness as he drew upon it. Another of the men let his fingers trail in the water, feeling the day's absorbed warmth still present on its surface, allowing water to trickle through his fingers, momentarily immersing himself in the gentle resistant tug. Then he withdrew his hand and wiped it dry on his trouser leg, thinking about how this was the easiest, best-paid job he had ever had.

Banu awoke to an unfamiliar noise. Since Pastor John had been taken she no longer slept as deeply as she once had. Even when she did sleep her dreams were disturbed by the images of what she had seen. The sound was getting louder, distant still, but closer, almost like the sound of a strong wind blowing through the treetops, yet different. Besides the trees were gone. Perhaps it was the ghosts of the trees calling out, asking not to be forgotten, or maybe seeking their revenge.

She crawled out from the little nipah shelter where she had made her bed. No one else had been awoken by the sound. A small amount of smoke still rose from the remaining embers of the evening's fire. Though it was dark Banu's eyes were keen. If she climbed a tree she might be able to see what was causing the approaching sound, or hide from the angry tree ghosts, if that's what the source of the sound was. She sensed a new coolness in the air around her, and the unmistakable smell of mud.

She shouted, hoping to wake the others in time, climbing now, not because it was something she had chosen to do, but because it was something her body had decided without asking her opinion, her bare legs gripping the rough bark of the tree as she climbed, heart pounding. The damp earthy smell drew all around her, the hissing roar almost deafening. She reached a crook in the tree and held tightly to the trunk as the loud glistening torrent flooded through the encampment, sweeping her sleeping family away, carried off in an impossible river of water and mud.

BANU STAYED in the tree until the sun came up. The unexpected river had only flowed for a few minutes, yet she couldn't bring herself to leave the safety of the tree until first light.

The encampment was gone, erased as surely as if it had never existed. She searched for any members of her family, but they were gone too, returned to the earth as she had predicted, not above the clouds as Pastor John had promised. The logger's cabin was gone as well, the loggers nowhere to be seen, the huge machines toppled on their sides, half-buried in the mud. She stayed, not knowing what else to do.

Then the machine appeared. At first she thought it was a bird, though it buzzed like an insect, hovering over the clearing, moving sharply away, then hovering again, as if surveying the wreckage. This machine had clearly come from the world beyond the forest, the world that had brought its destruction to this place, the world that had caused nature to turn against itself, taking everyone Banu had ever known and loved with it.

The first pebble missed, but Banu was a good shot. She loaded the sling again and the second pebble squarely hit its target. The machine jerked and tilted, then fell from the sky. She smashed it with a rock, not even taking the time to examine it or try to understand what it was or how it worked, but she took one of the blades from the tiny wreckage. It was hard and sharp enough to be a useful tool, while serving as a reminder.

Banu turned and left the wasteland, making her way to the forest's edge, taking the barely discernible trails that led deeper into its heart, following tracks mostly made by animals, knowing that sooner or later they would lead to water, whether a stream or a pond or a spring. She recognised familiar trees and plants along the way, instinctively noting their locations, knowing what was useful, what was edible, what was to be avoided.

She walked for three days, stopping only at night to sleep in the safety of trees, after checking them for snakes, putting distance between her and the past, between her and the world beyond the forest, leaving behind the world of men, yet fearing that it would soon find her.

Before you go

Though my name is on the cover, no book exists without the dedication and passion of a team of people working behind the scenes. The book you are holding in your hands (or perhaps reading on your screen) is the tropical fruit of the efforts of many people besides myself.

Reviews help persuade the reading community to give any books a shot.

Reviews help support writers and publishers.

This book is the result of years of work. I would be very appreciative if you could take less than a minute to leave a one-line review on a major online retailer in the USA or UK, or on Goodreads. More than one line would be fantastic too.

Also, feel free to rant or rave about *Lime Pickled* on the socials.

A very big thank you to you the reader, for whom this book was written.

Be happy,

Marc

Afterword

The stories in this collection are the tropical fruit of a decade and a half spent in Malaysia. A good number of these stories have been previously published elsewhere, sometimes in a slightly different form, while a few are appearing in print for the first time in this collection.

Anyone who has paid close attention to current affairs in Malaysia in the recent past will recognise a good many themes, references, and influences in these stories, but while some of these stories may have been inspired by real people and real events, they are entirely fiction, and the version of Malaysia that appears in these stories is also fictionalised, even if some of the settings do exist in the real world. For some readers, these stories may represent a rather bleak vision of the country. For this I make no apology.

The darkness that runs through these stories is informed by events I witnessed, sometimes up close, sometimes from a distance. My fifteen-year affair with the country had its share of ups and downs, and my faith in humanity was often shaken.

My time in Malaysia was also, like anything in human life, a subjective experience. I don't claim, indeed I can't claim, to 'know' Malaysia. But I have experienced it. I have observed it up close. I have listened and watched, sometimes, perhaps even often, with the detached perspective that comes with being a foreigner in a foreign land, a perspective that comes from having been an immigrant and emigrant my entire adult life, not so much an outsider looking in, but an inside outsider simply looking.

Malaysia is also a country that is changing fast. Very fast. The country to where I arrived in early 2007 is not the same country I left in 2022. Some of those changes have been for the good, some more problematic. The country's dynamism is one of its major strengths, but it can also be a shifting quicksand that can pull any unwary person down.

When I first arrived in Malaysia I lived in an unglamorous low-rise block of low-cost flats in an area wedged between Kuala Lumpur's Old Klang Road and the polluted Klang River. The neighbourhood was a joyless mould-stained concrete place, infested with rats and cockroaches, a place where crows stole clothes hangers to build plastic nests in blackened smog-stained trees, a place of open drains filled with dark foul-smelling oily water flecked with decomposing rice.

Drug dealers owned the stairwell of the building where I lived, beefy dark-skinned men who spoke in Tamil and had a steady flow of stumbling agitated customers every night. The only white person I ever saw was in the mirror, and though the dealers never hassled me, they eyed me, like everyone else who crossed their path, with suspicion.

It was a dengue neighbourhood. The dreaded breakbone fever was my welcoming gift, transmitted by the quivering kiss of an infected mosquito. I tried to sweat it out at home, but was eventually hospitalised. Not knowing if I could trust a government hospital, I gave almost half my savings to pay for a barrage of pointless tests and air-conditioned luxury in a well-known private hospital in nearby Petaling Jaya.

I came home after a few days, depressed and significantly poorer. The night of my return I woke from a fitful sleep to the sounds of shouts and screams just outside my window. Keeping the light off, I peeked down through the slats of the louvred window. The dealers stood over a skinny man who lay curled up in a ball, his arms protecting his head as kicks and swung motorcycle helmets rained down.

I wanted to call the police. My wife advised against it. The last time someone in the neighbourhood had called the police all the cars had their windscreens and headlights smashed. One man, the suspected caller, was only saved from the sharp blades of the gangster's parangs by the locked metal grill on his front door. He and his family quickly moved out of the neighbourhood and were never seen again. After that no one dared call the police.

A week later, a couple of hundred metres from where I lived, a big blue sports bag was found at the staircase near a book distributor's premises in a block of shop lots. Later, CCTV footage showed a motorcyclist leaving the bag there. Inside was a child's body, a little girl. She was identified as Nurin Jazlin. She was eight years old and had been missing for almost a month. The lurid details of her autopsy were stomach-churning. Nurin had been brutally tortured and sexually abused. It was a story that shook the nation. The Malaysian police even sought help from the FBI to enhance CCTV images. This led to the arrest of five people, but they were all later released, allegedly due to lack of evidence.

These were strong first impressions of Malaysia-Truly-Asia. Apparently, the modern Asian Tiger I had read and heard so much about was a violent blood-thirsty beast. I seriously contemplated giving up and leaving. Instead, after much debate, my wife and I decided to change neighbourhood.

We didn't go very far, just a few hundred metres away, but crossed the invisible border between the Federal Territory of

Kuala Lumpur into Petaling Jaya. Though it was close to our previous abode, our new home was quite different. Instead of drug dealers, there was an air-conditioned gatehouse with Nepali security guards in neat uniforms. Our apartment looked over a shining blue swimming pool bordered with coconut palms and frangipanis. Aunties practised Tai Chi and Qi Gong in the mornings, and the evenings were punctuated by the pock of tennis balls from the tennis court. In short, a luxurious situation that would only be accessible to the ultra-rich in Europe, but that in Malaysia was still considered relatively accessible and affordable.

I settled more comfortably into my new life in Malaysia in these surroundings. I swam almost every day, and learned the joys of air-conditioning, while hammering away at my laptop, transcribing the previous three years' worth of journals written between travels in India and summers spent in a remote hut at the foot of a glacier in the French Pyrenees National Park. I dreamed of being a writer, or more to the point, a published writer. The resulting 180,000-word manuscript still gathers dust in the dark recesses of my hard drive.

But it wasn't all love and light. The neighbours got hot and bothered, their disputes occasionally further fuelled by the beer and whiskey that flowed freely in the little restaurant downstairs by the poolside. In the evenings I could stand on my balcony and see half a dozen domestic disputes going on at any given time: husbands shouting at their wives, wives screaming at their maids, maids shouting at the children when the parents weren't around, the children taking it out on each other as they fought amongst themselves. I lost count of the number of times I saw parents cane their children, bringing back sour sharp memories of my school days in Ireland. But somehow, over time, the shouting and arguing just became background noise, like the distant traffic or the caws of the bellicose crows.

At first I was friendly with the residents and chatted with the elderly Chinese aunties, stocky rectangular women who whiled away their hours gossiping by the pool or engaged in raucous noisy games of Mah Jong. They wore their grey hair short and had a dress code of floral-print polyester trouser suits. Their leader was a stern woman – let's call her Madam Tan. All the other women deferred to her alpha-female status and constantly sought her much-withheld approval. There were seven eight-storey buildings in the compound. According to these aunties a cloud of 'dark energy' hung over one of them – of course, the building where I lived. For proof they offered the anecdote of one of my upstairs neighbours moving out because she had heard a 'voice' telling her to jump from the sixth-floor balcony.

Though I lived on the fourth floor, the label in the elevator assured me that I lived on 3A. The number 4 in Chinese sounds similar to the word for 'die' or 'death' and to say there is a lot of superstition around the number is an understatement. The fact that my apartment was also number 4 made it difficult to rent, and it had been empty for some time before we moved in. A sign over the doorway repeated the deadly digit: Apartment 4-4. Apartment Die-Die. Apartment Double-Death.

In an attempt to neutralise the maleficent effects of the numbers, our landlady had added the Chinese character for Fatt, meaning good luck and prosperity, which sounds similar to the word for 8.

I didn't give any credence to these homonymous and numerological superstitions, but the aunties insisted I was doomed. I didn't care for discussions on the matter and told them so. This led to a certain falling out between the aunties and myself, further compounded by my refusal to sign their petition to have some African football players evicted from the next building for having the temerity to be black (an episode which some faithful readers might recognise as being the inspiration for the story All I Want to do is Play Football, featured in my first short story collection, Tropical Madness). I no longer stopped at the benches for chats on my way to and from the pool, but still nodded and smiled in a neighbourly way.

And so life went on. I swam, I wrote, I sweated in the ever-present humid heat, hammering away at my work-in-progress in apartment Double-Death.

It was an evening like any other evening, until it wasn't, until it became an evening unlike anything I have ever known before or since. My wife was out and I kept writing through the evening, so engrossed in my transcriptions that I barely registered the blaring call for prayer at sunset from the nearby mosque. At some stage I became aware of a man wailing and moaning in one of the apartments nearby. I assumed he was drunk and silently cursed him for distracting me from my writing.

A while later my flow of thoughts and words was interrupted by the hum of chattering conversation. I guessed the residents were having one of their regular poolside parties, celebrating a birth, marriage, or a perhaps a birthday. These events were quite regular. Plastic awnings were erected poolside and buffet tables laden down with exotic dishes that filled the air with the aromas of lemongrass and lime leaves, curries and fermented fish, and sometimes, depending on the party, bottles of hard liquor and cooler boxes of iced beer. I was occasionally invited to these gatherings, but I generally declined, not always relishing the role of being the token white guy, using the excuse that I was vegetarian, which was true, and that I didn't drink, which was mostly true. No one had invited me to a poolside party that evening, though there was nothing unusual in that, but the distracting thoughts of those fragrant dishes brought water to my mouth, dragging me away from my manuscript and into the kitchen.

In contrast to anywhere I have ever lived in Europe, every

door and window in every apartment in the block was equipped with bars and grilles. Despite the relative luxury, I sometimes felt like I was caged in an upscale prison, or a sort of human zoo. There was no glass in the kitchen window, just a metal grille. The chattering of conversation was louder there, which was unusual because the kitchen faced the opposite side of the building from the swimming pool. The unseen man was still howling. His roars were inconsolable. He was clearly a good deal more distressed than the average drunk.

I heard the crackle of a walkie-talkie. Through the window bars I saw five or six policemen on the landing in front of the elevator, each side of which were four apartments. The police were focused on the apartment that mirrored mine on the other side of the landing. They talked in hushed tones into handheld radios and amongst themselves.

I was curious but didn't want to talk to them, since I suffer from a chronic condition that involves a deeply ingrained antipathy towards men in uniforms, and men in uniforms who carry guns in particular. In any case the policemen didn't notice me looking out the window. Or if they did, they ignored me.

Given the abject anguish apparent in his voice I thought perhaps the wailing man was suicidal. A jump from the fourth floor would probably have been enough to do the job. Maybe the police were debating how to rescue him. I finished stir-frying my improvised dish of oyster mushrooms, tofu, and fresh baby sweetcorn, and went out to the balcony at the other end of the apartment to eat in the relative cool of the night air.

The chattering was louder there. I leaned over the railings and saw a crowd gathered below. This added fuel to my imagined scenario of suicide. From their angle they might have been able to see him. Some people pointed up at me, chattering excitedly. This made me think that they couldn't see my distressed neighbour after all. I quickly withdrew my head. Something was up, that much was certain, but I didn't want to ask the policemen outside my door, nor go downstairs and join the rubbernecking crowd. Meanwhile the man kept wailing.

I called my wife to let her know what was going on. When she got back home she told me that yellow plastic crime-scene tape was strung across the front of our building. There were more policemen downstairs. She ignored the tape, walked past the policemen, and came up in the elevator. No one stopped her and she didn't ask what was going on.

Sometime later the man stopped wailing. It was late. The crowd of disappointed spectators slowly drifted away.

The following morning the doorbell rang. Two young ladies with clipboards introduced themselves as journalists from a major English language daily. I never suspected at the time that I would one day become a regular contributor to the book review section of that same stellar newspaper, but for several years I gladly occupied that post. Meanwhile, the journalists at my doorstep asked me if I could tell them anything about the murders. This was the first I heard about the double death.

Afterwards, I wondered why the police never knocked on my door. Surely it was standard crime scene investigation procedure to ask neighbours if they had seen anything suspicious. Not that I could have told them anything useful in any case.

The details came out in the local press over the next few days, and from the gossiping, petitioning aunties, who were suddenly eager to talk to the white man who lived in apartment Double-Death again.

The wailing man had come home from work around nine-thirty in the evening to find the security gate of his apartment unlocked. Inside his wife and three-year-old son lay dead. There was blood everywhere. The mother's face had been lacerated. The boy had lost an ear. They had both been stabbed repeatedly.

At first the police couldn't find the murder weapon, or rather they just found part of it, the handle. Later they found the rest of the knife buried deep inside the woman's ribcage.

There were no signs of a forced entry. No valuables or cash

had been taken. This led the police to surmise that the woman must have known her killer. Apart from the broken knife and a few bloody footprints there were no other leads – no fingerprints, no witnesses, no clues, other than the fact that the killer had apparently taken the time to shower, and presumably change clothes.

The broken knife suggested frenzied violence in the repeated stabbing of the mother and also led me to the uneasy conclusion that the boy was murdered first. Their final moments must have been utterly terrifying.

I knew them both to see. We often shared the elevator. The boy was of an age where he would look at my white skin with curiosity, but elevators are awkward spaces and silence is often the unspoken rule. There's an incident in my head, that may be real or not, where I say hello to the little boy and his mother tells her son to "Say hello to Uncle." To the best of my knowledge, beyond that we never had any other contact. Like my wife and I, our neighbours kept to themselves.

I found it hard to accept, and still find it hard to accept, that all this happened while I was sitting just a few metres away. I searched my memory for details. Had I heard the woman scream? Had I heard the little boy cry out? Perhaps, but if I did it didn't register in any meaningful way, such sounds being sadly not uncommon.

The man moved out, of course. The police quickly cleared him of any suspicion. He had strong alibis, no motive, and the authenticity of his grief was unmistakable. Some neighbours installed new security gates and cameras, while others came to burn incense, pray, and leave offerings outside the victims' apartment. For months the yellow and black crime-scene tape stayed fastened to the metal grille. Even when it was eventually removed, the apartment remained unoccupied.

To the best of my knowledge, the killer was never found. If so, it was never reported in the press, and the gossiping aunties would have been only too pleased to share the news with me if the perpetrator had been caught. Though they did tell me that one of my neighbours – a 'foreigner' – had disappeared the same day.

Things returned to normal. The African footballers had been safely evicted and Madam Tan, who was talking to me again, eagerly repeated her ominous warnings about the curse on the building where I lived. She advised me to move out. Now that the dark energy of death had come it would never leave.

I told her I didn't believe in such things. Then our immediate next-door neighbour, a man in his sixties, who spent hot days sweating over a boiling cauldron of soup in the hawker centre across the road, and was said to make the best won-ton noodles in the area, dropped dead, apparently of a heart attack.

Madam Tan sternly waggled her forefinger at me every time I passed, as if to say 'watch out, you'll be next.' She even forecast that I would be struck by lightning while swimming in the condominium's pool.

Incredible though it might seem she wasn't far wrong. Shortly thereafter I did get hit by lightning, though not in the swimming pool, but at a waterfall near Rawang. I was standing in a puddle of water when the lightning struck. Thankfully it wasn't a direct hit, but it still took almost a year for me to fully recover the feeling in my feet, and ever since I can walk on sharp-stoned reflexology footpaths without the slightest discomfort.

A brief holiday on the island of Langkawi convinced me that there were parts of Malaysia that were more peaceful and bucolic than our seemingly blighted neighbourhood, and soon we set plans in motion to leave the mainland for a new island life. Our landlady, a serious young woman in her thirties, accepted our decision to move out, though confessed that she was worried if she would ever find new tenants, given the gruesome murders next door, the wonton uncle's death, and the unlucky double number 4 over the doorway.

She didn't have to worry long. Four months later she was dead.

Witnesses said the accident was a mystery. She had been driving to work and inexplicably swerved, crashing into the metal divider in the middle of the highway. It went straight through the windscreen, killing her instantly, leaving behind a widower and three small children.

Though this reads like an exaggerated litany of death, these are the things I think of when I look back on just the first years of my time in Malaysia and my time living in apartment Double-Death. I would rather it were fiction. Sadly it is not. Did I allow these incidents to blight my view of Malaysia? Of course I did, but I was willing to try again, in a different setting.

I won't bore the reader with all the dark details of what happened in Langkawi. I will quickly pass by the number of heroin-addicted neighbours who overdosed. I won't describe the numerous acts of corruption perpetrated at almost every interaction I had with officialdom. But I will say I never caved. I never paid a single bribe, a choice that made my life significantly much more difficult than it might otherwise have been.

But Malaysia opened doors and opportunities for me that I am unlikely to have had elsewhere. My writing started to be published and I was made to feel welcome into Malaysia's relatively small writing scene, finding a sense of community among fellow readers and writers, attending the yearly George Town Literary Festival in Penang with avid fervour, and sometimes even being invited to participate in events. Living in Malaysia allowed me to publish my first book, and now my time spent there has enabled me to follow it up with this collection you hold in your hands. For these things and many more I am grateful.

After more than ten years in Langkawi we decided to move to Penang, where I would be able to enjoy, and possibly participate in the vibrant local cultural scene.

Barely a few weeks after we moved the first MCO, or lock-down, was announced. Like millions of other people in Malaysia we hardly left our home for two years. Like millions of others we lost our main source of income. Luckily we had some savings. The proverbial rainy day had arrived. Every sector of society was feeling the pinch. I lost most of the few writing jobs I had. Then a local publisher approached me with a top-secret project. Non-disclosure agreements were signed. I had acted as a freelance editor and proofreader for this publisher several times, working on a variety of books, mostly non-fiction, several with a historical or political slant. I was grateful for the work. For this project I acted simply as proofreader. The book went on the become a bestseller, but it also caused some rather large waves. One of those waves brought officers of Malaysia's notorious Special Branch to my door. Throughout the four-hour interrogation they were very polite and professional and made clear to me that I wasn't the one under investigation, but the author. They made it even clearer that I should not continue editing or proofreading books of this nature for this or any other publisher in Malaysia.

A few weeks later, by sheer coincidence, in obviously absolutely no way whatsoever related to the interrogatory visit from the gentlemen of Bukit Aman, I was informed that my work permit would not be renewed, which was sort of ironic since I no longer had any work in any case. After fifteen years in Malaysia I was still no closer to obtaining permanent resident status that would have made work permits unnecessary. And so it was that I had to face up to the all-too-evident fact that there was no future for me in Malaysia.

I had always planned to leave eventually, though I didn't expect it to be under these circumstances. I got my vaccine booster shot, my PCR test results, and said my goodbyes to a land that has played a huge part in my life, a land I tried and struggled to accept, a land that sometimes tried to accept me. I left with a lot of mixed feelings. I left with a sour taste in my mouth. But for better, or for worse, I spent a significant portion of my life in Malaysia, and the stories in this volume are part ode and part elegy to that.

Marc de Faoite

Acknowledgments

Many people played a role in supporting or even just tolerating me in the process of writing this collection of stories. First among them is Meng Foong, who I'd like to thank for always giving me the space and time to write and for providing the endless mugs of tea, sandwiches, and bowls of super-spicy Korean noodles that were consumed along the way. To my parents, Noel and Siobhan for life and so much more. To Tanya and Colin and Emma. To Evan and Hazel and Lucy and Chloe. To Jen/Ber, Chikoyo, John, and Dave. To Pat, who should have had his own TV show. To my aunts and uncles and cousins spread all over the world. To Sharon for being a tireless friend and mentor. To Gareth, and all the team at Gerakbudaya, for his constant support. To Amir. To Minh and Malini and Sharmilla and Shazmin and Eric, to Bettina and Shireen and Viji, and anyone else who provided a home for my writing over the years. To my writing buddies Connla, Preeta, Elaine, Damyanti, thank you so much for your encouragement and your insights which have made me a better writer and this a better book. To Brigitte and Malachi Edwin and Shivani. To Alan and Sharon and Oisin and Shona and Siobhan and Anita and all the rest of the Brussels crew. To Valerie for throwing me a lifeline. To my colleagues Lhundup and Diogo with whom I share the vampire shift. And a very special thanks to Ivy Ngeow and Josh Lee at Leopard Print for accepting this manuscript in its raw form and for all the hard work that went into making it more presentable, without whom you wouldn't be reading this. Thank you.

About the Author

Born in Dublin, Marc de Faoite is a freelance writer and editor. Based in Malaysia from 2007 to 2022, he regularly reviewed books for The Star and The Vibes. He now lives at the foot of the French Alps. He was runner-up for The D.K. Dutt Award for Literary Excellence in both 2015 and 2016, and runner-up for the inaugural Fay Khoo Award for Food and Drink Writing in 2016. *Tropical Madness*, a collection of his short stories, was longlisted for the 2014 Frank O'Connor International Short Story Prize.

You can find him at
Twitter: @marcdefaoite
Websites: www.marcdefaoite.com
www.globalscribesolutions.com
Goodreads: https://tinyurl.com/MarcdeFaoite
Author page
email: marcdefaoite@gmail.com

Publication Credits

Several of the stories featured in this collection have previously been published elsewhere, albeit in some instances in slightly different form.

- *Seed* was published in Rambutan Literary, and in a slightly different form by Word Works in Everything About Us.
- *Lime Pickled* was published in Kisah Journal.
- *Big Balls* was runner up for the DK Dutt Memorial Award For Literary Excellence and published by Word Works in Champion Fellas.
- *Mutiny in Kampung Merokok* was published pseudonymously in Eksenrtika.
- *The Green Fuse* was published by Fixi Novo in Little Basket 2016.
- *Temptation* was published by Fixi Novo in Little Basket 2017.
- *The Girl With The Crooked Nose* was published Fixi Novo in Little Basket 2018.
- *Majestic Heights* was published by Fixi Novo in Love in Penang.
- *Joget Girl* was published by Fixi Novo in Hungry in Ipoh.
- *The Bamboo Swing* was published in Esquire Magazine (Malaysia).
- *Dr Fintan* was published in The Incubator.

- *MCO Manicure Control Order* was published in The Lockdown Chronicles, 2021
- *Banu* was published by Leopard Print in Asian Anthology New Writing Vol. 1: Stories by Writers from Around the World, 2022.

All other stories are previously unpublished.

Also by Marc de Faoite

SHORT STORY COLLECTION

Tropical Madness, published by Buku Fixi

SHORT STORIES

Banu (Asian Anthology New Writing Vol. 1, 2022)

Bedclothes for Beckett (The Blue Nib, May 2020)

Stan and me (Pendemic, April 2020)

Groceries for Lydia Davis (The Cormorant, December 2019)

Antecessor (Endings and Beginnings, November 2018, *Runner up for the 2017 D. K. Dutt Memorial Award For Literary Excellence)*

The Girl with the Crooked Nose (Little Basket- New Malaysian Writing, October 2018)

Scapefish (The Honest Ulsterman, June 2018)

The Lift (New Reader Magazine, issue 2, page 99, June 2018)

Find Yourself (Stories for Homes: Volume 2, November 2017)

Escargots de Bourgogne (Fay Khoo Award runner-up, October 2017)

Dr Fintan (The Incubator, issue 13, page 50), August 2017)

You Drive, first published as Temptation (Little Basket 2017: New Malaysian Writing, March 2017)

Lime Pickled (Naratif Kisah Journal, October 2016)

Saving Life the Five-Foot-Way (Anak Sastra Issue 24, 2016)

Apartment Double Death (Eastlit, September 2016)

The Year Our Voices Broke (Lakeview International Journal ofLiterature and Arts (pages 140-150), August 2016)

Seed (Everything About Us:Readings from Readings 3, August 2016)

Seed (Rambutan, June 2016)

Death or Plastic (The Runt: Lost at Sea #9, May 2016)

The Green Fuse (Little Basket: New Malaysian Writing, April 2016)

Big Balls (Champion Fellas, March 2016*) Runner up for the D. K. Dutt Memorial Award For Literary Excellence*

Finnuala Fiesta (The Incubator (pages 41-48), December 2015)

No Sa-Butti Soup (Dawn of a New Sky, November 2015)

Joget Girl (Hungry in Ipoh, October 2015)

Born Outside the Box (As Life Found Me, June 2015)

The Bamboo Swing (Esquire Magazine, Dec 2014)

Across the Square (Jotters United: Issue 3, 2014)

A Dynasty of Dust (Jaggery, Summer 2014)

Under the Shade of the Tamarind Tree (North East Review, April 2014)

Protection (Roadside Fiction, April 2014)

Ah Girl is in a Relationship (Esquire Magazine, January 2014)

Lorong Gelap (Popradeeo, October 2013)

Mamak Murder Mystery (KL Noir: Red, Fixi Novo, 2013)

Majestic Heights (Love in Penang, Fixi Novo, 2013)

Green Onions (Lost in Putrajaya, Fixi Novo, 2013)

Trapped in Traffic (Esquire Magazine, Feb 2013)

Milking Pen (Readings from Readings 2, Word Works, 2012)

Night Fishing (Readings from Readings 2, Word Works, 2012)

Last-time Kopitiam (Fish Eats Lion, Math Paper Press, 2012)

Lessons at the Night Market(Sini Sana:Travels in Malaysia, May 2011)

Lessons at Muthu's Barbershop (Sini Sana:Travels in Malaysia, May 2011)

CPSIA information can be obtained
at www.ICGtesting.com
Printed in the USA
BVHW080836240123
656976BV00005B/167